THE BREAD OF OUR EARLY YEARS

THE BREAD OF OUR EARLY YEARS

by

HEINRICH BÖLL

Translated by Mervyn Savill

ARCO PUBLICATIONS LIMITED
LONDON

The Bread of Our Early Years was first published in 1957 by
Arco Publications Limited, 10 Fitzroy Street, London, W.1

First Edition April, 1957

PRINTED AND BOUND IN GREAT BRITAIN BY
THE GARDEN CITY PRESS LIMITED,
LETCHWORTH, HERTFORDSHIRE

I

THE DAY HEDWIG ARRIVED WAS A MONDAY, and on that Monday morning, before my landlady pushed father's letter under the door, I should have preferred to pull the blanket up over my face, as I had so often done when I still lived in the apprentices' home.

But my landlady called out from the corridor: "There's a letter for you from home." When she pushed the letter under the door and it slipped snow white into the grey shadow in which my room still lay, I jumped up in terror from my bed because, instead of a round post office stamp, I had recognised the oval station franking.

Father, who hated telegrams, had only sent me two express letters in the seven years I had lived in the city; the first had announced Mother's death, the second Father's accident when he broke both legs—and this was the third. I tore it open and was relieved when I read it: "Don't forget," wrote Father, "that Muller's daughter Hedwig, for whom you found the room, arrives by train today at 11.47. Be nice, meet her, buy her a few flowers and be friendly. Try to imagine how such a young girl must feel: she's arriving in the city for the first time. She does not know the streets or the district where she will live; everything will be strange and the big crowded station at midday will terrify her. Think, she is just twenty and is coming to the city to be a school teacher. Pity you can't come and visit me regularly on Sundays, pity. Your affectionate Father."

. . . . .

Later I often wondered what would have happened had I not fetched Hedwig at the station. Just as one boards the wrong train I should have embarked on another life—a life which in the days before I met Hedwig had seemed to me quite tolerable. This is how I termed it whenever I mentioned it, but this life which awaited me like the train on the other platform, the train that one almost took—I live this life now in my dreams, and I know that what at that time seemed tolerable would have become a hell; I see myself leading that life, smiling, hearing myself speak, as in a dream one sees a twin brother smiling and hears him talk—the twin brother who perhaps was there for a split second, before the seed that bore him perished.

I was surprised that Father had sent me the express letter, and I did not know whether I should have time to fetch Hedwig, for since I had specialised in the repair and servicing of automatic washing machines, my weekends and Mondays were busy. On Saturdays and Sundays when the husbands were home from work, they tinkered about with the washing machines because they wanted to test the quality and functioning of these costly acquisitions, and I sat by the telephone and waited for calls which often took me to the outer suburbs. As soon as I entered their houses, I could smell burnt-out contacts or cables, or I found machines from which the foam gushed as in an animated cartoon, men with crushed fingers, weeping women who had forgotten to press or had pressed the few essential buttons twice. Then I enjoyed the indolence with which I opened my tool-bag, examined the damage with a sneer on my lips, busied myself peacefully with controls, levers and connections and set the regulation mixture of soap powder, explaining with a friendly smile how the machine ran, let it run and, while I washed my hands, listened politely to the amateurish remarks of the husband who liked to see his technical capabilities taken seriously. When I presented the bill with my time and expenses, they did not look at it too closely, and I got calmly into my car and drove to the next call.

Twelve hours' work, Sundays included, and an

occasional engagement with Wolf and Ulla in the Café Joos. On Sunday evenings Mass, at which I usually arrived late, and had to determine by the priest's movements whether the sacrament had already begun; and my sigh of relief when it had not begun, and I was tired and sometimes fell asleep in my pew and only woke up as the server's bell announced the transubstantiation. There were times when I hated myself, my work and my hands.

. . . . .

I was tired that Monday morning; there remained six calls from Sunday, and I heard my landlady in the hall saying on the telephone: "Yes, I'll tell him." I sat on the edge of the bed, smoking and thinking of Father.

I could see him walking through the town in the evening, delivering the express letter to the train which stops at Knochta at ten o'clock; I saw him cross the square to the church, past Muller's house, along the small avenue with the stunted trees; to take a short cut, he then opened the big gate of the Gymnasium, went through the dark entrance into the courtyard, looked up at the yellow-distempered back of the school building to his Lower First, past the tree in the middle of the courtyard which stank of the caretaker's dog.

I saw Father unlock the little gate which was left open every morning from five minutes to eight to eight o'clock for the country pupils who rushed across from the station, while Hohnscheid, the housemaster, stood by the gate to see that none of the children who lived in the city crept in through the country children's door. Alfred Gruhs, for example, the station-master's son, had to make his way round the whole block because he did not come in by train.

On summer evenings the sun was reflected red in the classroom window-panes. During my last year in Knochta, I often went this way of an evening with Father when we took letters or parcels for Mother to the train which came from the opposite direction and stopped at half-past ten in Brochen, where Mother lay in hospital.

Father usually returned by the same route through the school courtyard because it meant a saving of four minutes, saved him going round the ugly block of houses, and because he usually had a book or some exercise books to fetch. The memory of these summer Sunday evenings in the Gymnasium paralysed me—grey darkness lay in the corridors; a few lonely caps hung on the pegs outside the classrooms; the floor had been freshly beeswaxed; the silver bronze on the war memorial gleamed dully near the large snow-white square where the picture of Hitler had once hung, and Scharnhorst's collar gleamed blood red near the teacher's study.

I once tried to filch a stamped good-conduct certificate which lay on the table, but it was so solemn and stiff and rustled so loudly when I folded it and tried to put it under my shirt that Father, who stood near the bookshelf, turned round, snatched it angrily out of my hand and threw it back on the table. He did not try to smooth it out or scold me, but from then onwards I had to stay outside in the corridor and wait for him, alone with Scharnhorst's blood-red collar, alone with the red lips of Iphigenia, whose picture stood near the Upper First, and all that remained to me was the dark grey gloom in the corridor and an occasional look through the peep-hole into the Upper First. But I could see nothing through the peep-hole except grey darkness. Once I found an ace of hearts on the freshly polished floor; it was the same red as Iphigenia's lips and Scharnhorst's collar, and beneath the odour of the fresh beeswax I could smell the school cooking. Outside the classroom I could clearly see the round traces left by the hot canister on the linoleum, and this smell of soup, the thought of the canister which stood on Monday midday outside our classroom, aroused my hunger, which the red of Scharnhorst's collar, the red of Iphigenia's lips and the red of the ace of hearts could not silence.

On the way home I asked Father to look in and say "Good evening" to Fundahl the baker, and at the same time to ask for a loaf or the remains of the dark grey cake, whose layer of jam was as red as Scharnhorst's collar. As we walked home through the dark silent streets, I ran over the whole conversation Father should have with Fundahl so as to make our visit seem accidental. I was surprised at my own ingenuity, and the nearer we came to Fundahl's shop the more vivid became my imagination and the better the imaginary dialogue which Father should have with Fundahl. Father shook his head energetically, because Fundahl's son was in my class and a lazy pupil, and when we reached the baker's house he stood there hesitating for a moment; I knew how difficult it was for him, but I persisted, and Father always made one of those clumsy turns such as soldiers make on the films, went over to the door and rang Fundahl's bell. Ten o'clock on Sunday night and the silent scene was always repeated—someone opened the door, but it was never Fundahl himself, and Father was too embarrassed and too excited to even say "Good evening," and Fundahl's son, his daughter or his wife, whoever came to the door, would call into the dark corridor: "Father, it's the school teacher," and Father waited in silence while I stood behind him taking in the smell of Fundahl's supper. There was a smell of roast or fried bacon, and when the cellar door was open I could smell bread. Then Fundahl appeared, went into the shop and fetched a loaf, which he handed unwrapped to Father, and Father took it without a word. The first time, we had neither briefcase nor paper with us, and Father carried the bread home under his arm while I walked in silence at his side watching the expression on his face. It was always a serene, proud expression and no one could see how difficult it had been for him. When I tried to take the bread and carry it, he shook his head amiably, and after this, when we went to the station on Sunday evening to send our parcels to Mother, he always took care that we had a briefcase with us. There were months in which I already began to look forward to this loaf on Tuesday, until one Sunday Fundahl himself opened the door and I saw at once from his face that we should get no bread. His big black eyes were hard, his chin was like the face of a statue and he hardly moved his lips as he said: "I can only sell bread and I cannot sell it on Sunday evening." He shut the door in our faces, the same door which today is the entrance to his café, where the local jazz club holds its sessions. I have seen the red poster—a smiling negro with his lips pressed to the gold mouthpiece of a saxophone.

It had only taken us a few seconds to pull ourselves together and go home, I with the empty brief-case whose leather was as limp as a shopping bag. Father's face was as proud and serene as ever. "I had to give his son bad marks yesterday," he said.

. . . . .

I heard my landlady grinding coffee in the kitchen, heard her gently reprimanding her small daughter, and I still felt an urge to get back to bed and pull the blankets over my head. I recalled how wonderful it had been in the old days; in the apprentice's home I had known how to look dejected so that the principal, Chaplain Derichs, would order me to stay in bed with tea and a hot-water bottle; when the others had gone down to breakfast I fell asleep again and only woke up at eleven o'clock when the charwoman came to sweep the dormitory. Her name was Wietzel and I was afraid of her steely blue eyes and her powerful capable hands, and while she tidied the sheets and folded the blankets—avoiding my bed as though I were a leper—she always uttered that warning which still echoes in my ears today: "You'll never be any good, you'll never be any good." Her compassion when Mother died and everyone was kind to me—

her compassion was even worse. . . . After Mother's death, when I changed my calling and my classroom, and idled for days on end in the home, until the Chaplain found me a new job—I peeled potatoes or wandered round the corridors with a broom—in those days her compassion had vanished once more, and as soon as she caught sight of me she uttered her dark prophecies: "You'll never amount to anything." I was afraid of her and fled as from an angry, pecking bird into the kitchen, where I felt safe under Frau Fichter's protection; I helped her cook the cabbage and earned myself many an extra helping of pudding because I grated the big cauliflower heads and let myself be lulled to sleep by the kitchenmaid's songs. When she sang, certain lines had to be hummed, lines which Frau Fichter considered immoral, such as: "and he loved her in the vast black night." But the pile of white cauliflowers diminished quicker than I thought, and then followed two more dreadful days which I had to spend under Frau Weitzel's orders with my broom in my hand. Then the Chaplain found me a job with Wickweber, and after being a banking apprentice, a salesman's apprentice and a joiner's apprentice, I began as a junior electrician at Wickweber's.

Recently—I left the apprentice's home seven years ago—I met Frau Weitzel at a bus stop. I stopped my car and offered her a lift into the town. She accepted, but when I set her down outside her house she said amiably: "Thank you very much, but having a car doesn't mean that you've amounted to anything. . . ."

I did not pull the blankets over my head and refrained from deciding whether Frau Weitzel had been right, for it was a matter of indifference to me whether I had amounted to anything or not.

. . . . .

I was still sitting on the edge of my bed when my landlady brought in the breakfast. I gave her Father's letter to read while I poured out my coffee and buttered my roll.

"Of course you'll go," she said, laying the letter on the tray next to the sugar basin. "You must be nice and invite the girl to have something to eat. Remember, most of these young girls are hungrier than they'll ever admit."

She left the room because the telephone rang, and once more I heard her say: "Yes, I'll tell him." When she came back, she said: "It's a woman from the Kurbelstrasse. She was weeping because she could not get her machine going. She begs you to come at once."

"I can't," I replied. "I must finish yesterday's calls first."

My landlady shrugged her shoulders and left the room. I finished my breakfast, washed, and thought of Muller's daughter whom I did not know. She was to have come to the city in February, and I had laughed at her father's handwriting, at his letter which from my small knowledge of English I knew had been censored, and his style.

"My daughter Hedwig," Muller wrote, "is coming to town in February to begin her studies at the Teacher's Academy. I should be grateful if you could help me to find a room for her. I am sure that you will not remember me. I am the principal of the Hoffman von Fallersleben School, where you spent some years as a boy"—in this elegant manner he stressed that, at the age of sixteen, after twice failing to get my remove into the Fourth, I had left the school as a failure in the Lower Third—"so perhaps," Muller went on, "you will remember me, and I hope that my request will not cause you too many difficulties. The room for my daughter should be not too ostentatious and yet not too ugly, not far from the Teachers' Academy and if possible not in a slum district, but I should like to stress that it must in any case be cheap." On reading this letter, Muller became quite a different person from my memory of him. I had looked upon him as easy-going and forgetful, a little slovenly perhaps, but now he seemed to be a pedant and a stickler, which did not fit in with my memory of him.

The word "cheap" had been enough to make me hate him, although I cannot remember him as having been hateful, for I loathe the word "cheap." Father, too, can tell stories of the days when a pound of butter cost one mark and a furnished room with bed and breakfast ten marks, the days when you could take a girl out dancing with thirty pfennigs in your pocket. In connection with stories of these days the word "cheap" was always uttered in a reproachful undertone as though it were the fault of the person to whom the story was being told that butter was now four times as dear. I had to learn the price of everything, because I could count—when I came to the city as a sixteen-year-old apprentice. Hunger taught me the prices; the thought of newly baked bread made my head swim, and I often strolled for hours of an evening through the city thinking of nothing but bread. My eyes smarted, my knees were weak and I felt that there was something wolfish in me. Bread. I hankered for bread as one hankers for morphia. I was afraid of myself and constantly thought of the man who in the apprentices' home had once given us a lantern-slide lecture on a North Pole expedition. He told us that they had ripped open live fish and eaten them raw. Even now, when I have money and am walking through the town with notes and coins in my pocket, I am overcome by the memory of the wolfish fear of those days and I buy bread which has just been put into the baker's shop window. I buy two of the most beautiful loaves and then a third in the next shop, and little crisp brown rolls—far too many, which later I leave in my landlady's kitchen, for I cannot eat a quarter of the bread I have bought, and the thought that bread can go mouldy fills me with anxiety.

My worst period was the months after Mother's death. I had no desire to pursue my studies or to become an electrician, but I had already tried so many other things. I had been a banking apprentice, a salesman's apprentice and a joiner's apprentice, all of them for exactly two months. And I hated my new profession and my master so much that I was often dizzy when I returned at night in the crowded tram to the apprentices' home. But I went on with my classes because I had decided "to show them." Four evenings a week I was allowed to visit St. Vincent's Hospital where one of Mother's distant relatives was cook; I was given soup and bread, and on the bench outside the kitchen door I sometimes found four or five other hungry people. Most of them were old men who stretched out their trembling hands to the hatch when it opened and Sister Clara's plump arm could be seen, and I had to control myself not to grab the bowl of soup out of her hands. This issue of soup always took place very late, long after the patients had gone to sleep. Sister Clara did not want to make them angry—as though an unseemly charity were being practised there—and in the corridor there were only two fifteen-watt bulbs to light our meal. Occasionally we were interrupted by the hatch being opened a second time as Sister Clara pushed through platefuls of pudding. The pudding was always red—as red as sticks of sugar candy at a fair—and when we rushed to the hatch Sister Clara stood there shaking her head and sighing, on the verge of tears. She said "wait," returned to the kitchen and brought a jug full of custard—sulphur-yellow custard, yellow as the sun in sunlit pictures—and we ate the soup, ate the pudding and the custard and waited to see whether the hatch would open again. Sometimes there was another slice of bread, and once a month Sister Clara distributed her cigarette ration to us. Each of us was given one or two of those precious white batons, but usually she only opened the hatch to tell us that she had nothing left. The groups that Sister Clara fed were changed each month, and then we belonged to another group with four visits allowed each week, and the fourth day was a Sunday. On Sundays there were sometimes potatoes and gravy, and I waited for the end of the month to be in this other group, with the desperate longing of a prisoner waiting for his release.

Since those days I have hated the word "cheap," because I always heard it on the lips of my employer. Wickweber was what people call a righteous man; he was capable, understood his craft and was good-natured in his own way. I was not quite sixteen when I joined him as an apprentice. He had two assistants and four apprentices in addition to a foreman, who usually worked in the small factory Wickweber had just founded. Wickweber was majestic, healthy and gay, and not even his piety could dull these traits. At the beginning I did not care for him, but two months later I hated him simply because of the odours that came from his kitchen. It smelt of things I had never tasted —newly baked cakes, roast meat and hot dripping, and Hunger, the beast that rampaged in my belly, could not bear these smells; it growled, and the bile rose hot and sour to my gorge, and I began to hate Wickweber because I came to work every morning with two slices of bread and jam and a mess-tin full of cold soup which I was supposed to warm up on some building site, but which I usually gulped down on my way to work. When I arrived at work, the empty mess-tin rattled in my tool-bag and I counted upon some woman customer bringing me bread, a plate of soup or something eatable. I was usually given something. At the time I was a tall, shy, silent ragamuffin and no one seemed to know that a wolf lived in my belly. I once overheard a woman say in a complimentary tone: "He looks so well bred." Fine, I thought, so I look well bred, and I began to gaze at myself more often in the mirror which hung in the lavatory in the apprentices' home. I gazed at my long pale face, made grimaces with my lips and thought: That's how you look when you're well bred. And I said aloud to my own face in the mirror: "I'd like something to eat. . . ."

Father always wrote that he would come one day and see how I was living, but he never came. When I went home he asked me what it was like in the city, and I had to tell him about the black market, the apprentices' home and my work, and he shook his head sadly, and when I mentioned my hunger—I did not mention it often, but sometimes it slipped out—Father went into the kitchen and fetched anything that was there to eat; apples, bread, margarine and sometimes he cut up slices of cold potatoes and fried them for me. But sometimes he returned helplessly from the kitchen with a red cabbage and said, "That's all I can find; I think one can make a salad out of it," but I never enjoyed the food. I had a feeling that I had committed a crime or expressed myself badly, describing conditions in the city in a way which did not represent the truth. I told him the price of bread, butter and cabbages, and each time he gave a start, but always seemed to forget. But he often sent me money and wrote that I should buy bread with it, and when the money came I went to the black market, bought myself a two- or three-pound loaf fresh from the bakery, sat down on a bench or somewhere among the ruins, broke the loaf in two and ate it with my dirty hands, tearing off pieces and stuffing them in my mouth. Sometimes it was warm and steamy inside, and for a moment I had the feeling of tearing a living being in my hands, and I thought of the man who had lectured on the North Pole expedition, who had told us that they had ripped open live fish and eaten them raw. I often wrapped part of the bread in a newspaper and stuck it in my tool-bag, but after walking a hundred yards I stopped, unpacked it, and swallowed the rest standing in the street. When it was a three-pound loaf I was so full that I gave my supper at the apprentices' home to someone else and went straight to bed. Alone in the dormitory upstairs I lay wrapped up in my blankets, almost comatose from satiety, my stomach full of sweet, new bread. It was eight o'clock in the evening, and I had eleven hours of sleep ahead of me; I could never get enough sleep. At the time Father was perhaps indifferent to everything except Mother's illness; in any case when I was at home I tried to avoid the word "hunger" and any hints as to my poverty, for I could see that Father had less to eat than I. He was yellow in the face, haggard and absent-minded. We went to visit Mother, and she also offered me things to eat as I sat at her bedside—things she had saved from her meals or had been given by visitors . . . fruit, a bottle of milk or a slice of cake, but I could not eat anything because I knew that she was consumptive and had to be well fed. But she urged me and said it would get stale if I did not eat it, and Father said: "You must eat, Clara; you must get well again." Mother wept, turned her face away, and I could not eat anything she offered me. In the next bed lay a woman in whose eyes I could see the wolf, and I knew that this woman would eat anything that Mother left, and I felt Mother's feverish hand on my arm and saw the fear of her neighbour's greed in her eyes. Mother gave me an imploring look and said: "Eat it, my dear boy, I know you're hungry and I know what it's like in the city." But I could only shake my head and squeeze her hand, silently begging her not to force me, and she smiled and did not mention the food again and I knew that she had understood.

"Perhaps you'd be better at home," I said. "Perhaps you'd be better in another ward." But Mother replied: "There isn't another ward, and they won't let me come home because I'm infectious." And later, when Father and I spoke to the doctor, I hated the doctor for his indifference. He was thinking of something else as he spoke to us; his eyes wandered to the door or to the window while he answered Father's questions, and I saw on his full red lips that Mother would die. But the woman who lay in the next bed died before Mother. When we came one Sunday afternoon she had just died; the bed was empty and her husband, who must have been sent for, came into the ward and began to collect her belongings in the wardrobe—hairpins, a compact, underclothes and a box of matches. He did it hastily and in silence without greeting us. He was small and thin and looked like a pike—a swarthy little man with little pig's eyes and when the sister on duty came in he shouted at her because he had not found a tin of meat in the cupboard. "Where's the corned beef?" he yelled at her. "I brought it to her yesterday . . . yesterday evening when I came from work, and if she died in the night she can't have eaten it." He brandished the hairpins before the sister's face and a yellowish foam appeared at the corners of his mouth. He kept screaming: "Where's the meat? I want the meat; I'll break up the whole bloody place if I don't get that tin of meat." The sister turned red and began to scream, and I thought that I could see in her face that she had pinched the meat. The fellow raged, flung things on the floor, stamped his feet and shouted: "I want that meat, you bunch of whores, thieves and murderers!" The scene lasted only a few seconds, for Father ran into the corridor to fetch someone, and I took up my position between the sister and the man because he had started to attack her. But he was small and agile, far quicker than I, and he managed to hit the sister with his small swarthy fists in the chest. He was snarling and showing his teeth in his rage; he reminded me of the rats I had seen, the rats which the kitchenmaids in the apprentices' home had caught in traps. "The meat, you bloody whore," he screamed, "the meat!" until Father came in with two male nurses who caught him by the scruff of the neck and dragged him into the corridor. But even through the closed door we could hear him screaming: "I want that meat, you thieves!"

We exchanged glances as soon as it was quiet

outside, and Mother said quietly: "Each time he came they quarrelled about the money she gave him to buy food. He always yelled at her and said that the prices had gone up, but she never believed him. It was terrible the things they said to each other, but she always gave him the money in the end." Mother fell silent, glanced at the dead woman's bed and said softly: "They'd been married for twenty years and they lost their only son in the war. Sometimes she took his photo from under the pillow and wept. It's still there with her money. He didn't find it, and as a matter of fact she did eat the meat." I tried to conjure up the picture of the dark-haired, greedy woman on the point of death, lying there that night in the bed next to Mother, eating the meat out of the tin.

. . . . .

Father wrote to me often in the years after Mother's death—ever more often, and the letters became longer. Usually he wrote that he would come and see how I was getting on, but he never came, and I lived seven long years alone in the city. After Mother's death he suggested that I should change my apprentice job and look for one in Knochta, but I wanted to stay in the city because I was beginning to find my feet and to learn

Wickweber's dodges, and I wanted to finish my time with him. I had also met a girl called Veronica; she worked in Wickweber's office; she was fair-haired and gay, and I spent a lot of time with her. On summer evenings we went for walks along the Rhine or ate ices, and I kissed her when we sat in the dark under the blue basalt stone of the quay wall, paddling our feet in the water. When the nights were bright and we could see across the river, we swam out to the wreck which lay in midstream and sat on the iron bench where the skipper had once sat on an evening with his wife. The cabin had long since been dismantled and we could only lean against an iron stanchion. The water gurgled beneath the ship. I met Veronica less often after she had been dismissed, when Wickweber's daughter took over the work in the office. A year later she married a widower who keeps a dairy not far from the street where I now live.

When my car is being overhauled and I have to travel by tram, I see Veronica behind her shop counter. She is still fair-haired and gay, but I can see the traces of the seven years which have passed in her face. She has grown fat and the children's washing hangs on a line in the courtyard—pink for a little girl and blue for a boy. Sometimes the door stands open and I see her behind the counter serving milk with her large beautiful hands. In the old days she sometimes brought me a loaf from one of her cousins who worked in a bakery. Veronica had taken it upon herself to feed me, and each time she gave me a piece of bread her hands were close to my eyes, and once I showed her Mother's ring and in her eyes I saw the same greedy light I had noticed in the eyes of the woman who lay in the bed next to Mother in the hospital. In those seven years I had enough experience of prices to appreciate the word "cheap"; nothing is cheap and the price of bread is still a trifle too high.

I found my feet, as they say, and I learnt my trade so well that I was no longer the cheap labour I had been for Wickweber for three years. I have a little car—it is even paid for—and long ago I saved up the guarantee which I have to pay to be released by Wickweber at any time and to be able to become one of his competitors. Most of the people with whom I have dealings are friendly and I am friendly to them. It is all quite tolerable. I have my own value, my own hands, my own technical knowledge, and my friendly approach to customers. (They extol my charm and my perfect manners, which have stood me in good stead, for I am also the representative for the washing machines which I have learnt to repair blindfold.) I have always been able to increase my value, everything is in the best of order, and in the meantime the price of bread has become stabilised, as they say. I worked twelve hours a day and slept eight, which left me four for what they call leisure. I met Ulla, my boss's daughter, to whom I was not officially engaged, but it was an understood thing that I should marry her. . . .

Sister Clara from St. Vincent's Hospital who gave me soup, bread, bright red pudding, sulphur-yellow custard and perhaps a dozen cigarettes—pudding which today I should not enjoy, and cigarettes I would no longer smoke—Sister Clara has long since been laid to rest in the convent cemetery. The memory of her sallow face and her sad, watery eyes when she finally had to close the hatch. . . . She deserves more tenderness than the others I met when I went out with Ulla. I read in their eyes, saw in their hands the price I should have to pay; I banished the spell, took away their clothes and their odours, all their cheap grandeur . . . and I roused the wolf that still slept in me, the hunger which taught me prices. I heard him snarl when at a dance I laid my head on a pretty girl's shoulder, and I saw the pretty little hand on my arm or resting on my shoulder turn to claws which had once deprived me of bread. Not many people gave me any presents—Father, Mother and sometimes the girls in the factory.

II

I WIPED MY RAZOR BLADE ON THE LOOSE-LEAF block which always hangs by the wash basin. The traveller from the soap firm gave it to me. The leaves are printed with a scarlet woman's mouth and below this scarlet mouth can be read: "Please do not wipe off your lipstick on your handkerchief." There are other blocks on which a man is cutting a handkerchief with a razor blade, and on these leaves is printed: "Use this paper for you razor blade." But I prefer to use the one with the scarlet mouth and give the others to my landlady's children.

I picked up the roll of wire which Wolf had brought the night before, picked up my money from the desk where I had emptied it out of my pocket, and as I left my room the telephone rang. Once more my landlady said: "I'll tell him!" Then catching sight of me she held out the receiver; I shook my head but she nodded so gravely that I went over and took it. A weeping woman's voice said something of which I only caught: "Kurbelstrasse . . . Come . . . please come." "All right," I said, "I'll come," and the weeping woman said something of which I only caught " . . . quarrel . . . My husband . . . Please come at once." And I repeated, "Yes, I'll come," and hung up.

"Don't forget the flowers," said my landlady, "and think of having a meal. It's nearly lunch-time."

I forgot the flowers. I drove back to town from an outlying suburb although I had a repair job to do in the neighbourhood and could thus have charged the mileage and the time twice. I drove fast because it was already half-past eleven and the train was due at 11.47. I knew this train; I often returned by it on Monday after visiting Father. On the way to the station I tried to imagine the girl.

Seven years ago, when I had spent the last year at home, I had seen her a few times; that year I had been exactly twelve times in Muller's house. A monthly visit to deliver the philology notebooks which it was my Father's turn to read. Clearly written on the bottom of the last page were the initials of the three philologists: MU for Muller, ZBK for Zubanek and FEN for my father, who had bequeathed me the name of Fendrich.

My clearest recollection was the dark stains on Muller's house; the damp had changed the green distemper into black clouds rising to the window of the ground floor; fantastic images which always seemed to me like maps out of some mysterious atlas. In the summer they dried as far as the edges and were surrounded by leprous white garlands, but even in the heat of summer the clouds retained a dark grey centre; in winter and autumn, the damp extended black and sour beyond these leprous edges like ink being absorbed by blotting paper.

I also recalled clearly Muller's slippered slovenliness, his long pipe, the leather bindings and the photographs in the corridor showing Muller as a young man in a bright-coloured student's cap. Beneath the photograph the scroll of Teutonia or some other "onia." Sometimes I had met Muller's son, who was two years younger than I. At one time he had been in my class, but he had long since outstripped me. He was raw-boned and looked like a young buffalo. He avoided remaining with me a moment longer than necessary, for he was a friendly chap. It was probably painful for him to be with me because he found it difficult to keep out of his voice all that I might have sensed in it—compassion, arrogance and that painful artificial joviality. So when he met me he confined himself to a hoarse "Good morning" and to showing me the way to his father's room. On two or three occasions I had seen a little girl of twelve or thirteen. The first time she had been playing with empty flower-pots in the garden; she had piled the bright red pots in the form of a pyramid against the moss-green wall; she gave a start when a woman's voice cried, "Hedwig," and her fear must have been communicated to the pile of flower pots, for the top one in the pyramid rolled down and broke on the wet dark concrete of the court-yard paving.

The second time, she had been in the corridor which led to Muller's room. She had arranged a laundry basket as a bed for her doll; corn-coloured hair fell down on her thin childish neck, which appeared almost green in the hall, and I heard her humming to the invisible doll an unfamiliar tune which was broken at certain intervals by a single word: Suweija-Su-Su-Su-Suweija. As I passed her on the way to Muller's room she looked up and I caught a glimpse of her face; she was pale and thin and her fair hair hung down in strands into her face. This must have been Hedwig, for whom I had now found a room.

Twenty thousand people at least in our city were looking for the type of room I had to find for Muller's daughter; only a couple of such rooms existed, rented by one of those unrecognised saints who occasionally wander on earth. I have such a room and I found it when I asked my father to take me away from the apprentices' home.

My room is large with a few old but comfortable pieces of furniture, and the four years I have lived in it seem to me an eternity. I have lived through the birth of my landlady's children and am godfather to the youngest, because it was I who went out into the night to fetch the midwife. For weeks on end I got up early, warmed Robert's milk and gave him his bottle, because my landlady, exhausted by her night shift, slept late in the morning and I never had the heart to wake her. Her husband is one of those men whom the world looks upon as an artist, when one of them is overwhelmed by circumstances; he complains for hours on end about his lost youth, which the war is supposed to have stolen from him. "We've been cheated," he says, "cheated of the best years of a man's life, the years between twenty and twenty-eight," and this lost youth serves him as an alibi for every possible stupidity, which his wife not only forgives him but makes possible. He paints, designs houses, composes. . . .

In my opinion he never does a good job, although now and again it brings him money. In the rooms of their flat hang some of his designs: "Residence for an author on the Taunushöhe"; "House for a sculptor," and on all these designs there are a host of trees drawn architecturally, and I hate architects' trees because I have seen them every day for five years. I swallow his counsels as one swallows medicine prescribed by a doctor of one's acquaintance: "In this city" is the gist of it—"I lived alone at about your age, and had to guard against dangers which I do not begrudge you." And I know that he means the brothel quarter.

My landlady's husband is very amiable but in my opinion a cretin, whose only virtue lies in retaining his wife's love and producing enchanting children. My landlady is tall and fair-haired, and there was a time when I was so much in love with her that I secretly kissed her apron and her gloves and could not sleep for jealousy of her cretinous husband. But she loves him and apparently a man does not need to be capable or successful to be loved and admired by such a woman. He often borrows a few marks from me to go to one of those artists' "dives" where he shows off his flowing tie and uncombed hair and drinks a whole bottle of gin. I give him the money because I cannot offend his wife by humiliating him. And he knows why I give him the money, for he has been endowed with that cunning without which good-for-nothings would die of hunger. He is one of those good-for-nothings who know how to give the impression of being a great improviser but I do not think he really knows how to improvise.

I always thought I had discovered a unique room, and I was therefore all the more surprised when I found one just as good for Muller's daughter in the centre of the town, in a house where I service the machines of a launderette. I check the insulation, put in new leads before they wear thin, and tighten the screws when they become loose. I love the centre of the city, the district which in the last fifty years has changed its proprietors and tenants like a dress suit—at first worn at a wedding, then by some impoverished uncle who earns a little extra money as a musician, and falls into disgrace in a pawnshop and is bought up at an auction sale by a dress hire shop, which lets it out reasonably to some hard-up gentleman who has suddenly been invited to a reception by some Minister, whose country their youngest son would look for in vain in an atlas.

In the house which is now a launderette, I found a room for Muller's daughter which complied with nearly all her fathers' stipulations; it was roomy and prettily furnished, with a large window overlooking an old patrician garden in the middle of the city; after five o'clock in the evening it was peaceful and quiet.

I rented the room from the 1st of February. Then I had difficulties because Muller wrote to me at the end of January that his daughter was ill and could not come before the 15th of March, and could I not see that the room was kept free without paying the rent. I wrote him an angry letter telling him of the housing situation in the city and then I was ashamed of myself because he wrote me a humble letter saying that he was prepared to pay the rent for six weeks.

I had hardly given a thought to the girl and had only made sure that Muller had paid the rent. He had sent it, and when I made inquiries the landlady asked me what she had already asked me when I inspected the room. "Is it your girl friend? Are you sure it's not your girl friend?"

"My God," I said irritably, "I told you, I don't know the girl."

"It's because I don't allow . . ."

"I know what you don't allow," I replied angrily, "but I've told you I don't know the girl."

"Good," she replied, and I hated her for her grin. "I'm only asking because sometimes I make exceptions for engaged couples."

"My God," I said, "I'm not engaged. Reassure yourself," but she did not seem reassured.

I arrived a few minutes late at the station, and while I put the coin in the automatic machine to buy a platform ticket I tried to recall the girl who in the old days had crooned "Suweija" when I carried the philology notebooks along the dark corridor to Muller's room. I stood on the stairs leading to the platform—fair-haired, twenty years old, coming to town to be a school teacher, and as I mustered the people who passed me it seemed as though the whole world was full of fair-haired twenty-year-old girls. So many of them stepped out of this train, and they all carried suitcases and looked as though they had come to the city to become school teachers. I was too tired to speak to any of them. I lit a cigarette and went to the other side of the stairs and saw a girl sitting on her suitcase behind the barrier, a girl who must have been sitting behind me all the time. She had dark hair, and her coat was as green as grass after a warm night of rain; it was so green that I thought it must smell of grass; her hair was as dark as sloping roofs after rain and her face as white as fresh distemper through which the ochre colour still shimmered. I thought she was made up, but I was wrong. I saw only this light green coat, this face, and suddenly I was seized by the fear explorers must feel when they land in a new country knowing that another expedition is on the way, and has perhaps already run up its flag and taken possession—explorers, who after the torments and efforts of a long journey, feared that their life-or-death struggle might have been in vain.

This face bored into me like a die, which presses

on wax instead of on silver bars, and I was transpierced without bleeding, and for one mad moment I had an urge to destroy this face, as an engraver might destroy the plate after taking a single impression from it.

I let fall my cigarette and ran up the six stairs. My fear vanished as soon as I stood before her. "Can I help you?" I asked. She smiled, nodded and replied: "Oh yes, can you tell me where the Judengasse is?"

"Judengasse," I repeated, and it was as though I had heard my name uttered in a dream without recognising it as my name. I was in the clouds and for the first time I seemed to understand what this expression meant.

"Judengasse," I repeated. "Yes, the Judengasse. Come with me." I was surprised to see her rise to her feet and pick up the heavy suitcase, and I was too bewildered to remember that I should be carrying it, too dazed to remember everyday courtesy —even when she said "Judengasse." I had not yet completely grasped the simple fact that she was Hedwig Muller. Something had changed or there had been some mistake. I was so convinced that Muller's daughter was fair-haired, that she was one of the countless fair-haired candidates for a teacher's post who had passed me, that I could not identify this girl with her, and even today I often wonder if she really is Hedwig Muller, and I utter this name with hesitation because I still think that I have to discover her identity. "Yes, yes," I replied to her questioning glance, "come along." And I let her go on ahead with her heavy suitcase and followed on her heels.

In this half a minute that I walked behind her I thought that I would possess her, and that if I did not possess her I would destroy everything that stood in my way. I saw myself breaking washing machines to pieces—smashing them with a ten-pound hammer. I stared at Hedwig's back, at her throat and at her hands which were bloodless from carrying the suitcase. I was jealous of the ticket collector who touched her hand for a moment as she handed him her season ticket, jealous of the very station platform on which she trod. I only thought of taking her suitcase just as we reached the exit. "Let me," I said, springing to her side and taking the suitcase from her hand. "It's nice of you to have come and met me," she replied.

"My God, don't you know me then?"

"Naturally," she said with a smile. "Your photograph is still on your father's desk."

"Do you know my father, then?"

"Yes, he used to teach me."

I put her suitcase and handbag in the back of

the car, and helped her in; for the first time I held her hand and elbow. It was round, powerful elbow and a large but gentle hand—a dry, cool hand—and as I walked round the car to get into my seat I stood in front of the radiator, opened the bonnet and pretended to inspect the engine, but in reality I was looking at her through the windscreen. I was afraid—no longer afraid that someone else would discover her and carry her off, that fear had vanished, because I would not leave her side, not today nor the many days to come, all those days which go to make up the sum of a lifetime. It was another fear, the fear of what was to come; the train I had wanted to take was ready to leave; it had steam up; my fellow passengers had already got in, the signals were down and the man with the red cap had already raised his flag; I was on the footboard and everything was now waiting for me to get in quickly, but at that moment I had already jumped off. I thought of the many frank conversations I should now have to bear, and I realised that I hated frank conversations—endless, pointless gossip, fruitless deliberations on guilt and innocence, reproaches, scolding, cries, letters, the guilt I should now shoulder, the guilt I already felt. I saw the second, quite tolerable life continue like a complicated machine, assembled for someone who was no longer there;

I was no longer there; the screws came loose, pistons seized up, bits of metal flew through the air and there was a smell of burning.

I had long since closed the bonnet, rested my arms on the radiator and looked through the windscreen at her face which was cut in two on the pane by the windscreen wiper. It seemed to me inconceivable that no man had yet noticed how beautiful she was; but perhaps she had not been beautiful until I had looked at her.

She glanced up at me as I got in and sat beside her, and in her eyes I saw the fear of what I should say or do. But I said nothing. In silence I started the car and drove into the city; from time to time when I turned to the right I could see her profile. I summed her up out of the corner of my eye, and she did the same. I drove to the Judengasse, had already slowed down the car outside the house where she was to live and pulled up at the house, but I did not know what to do when we stopped, got out and went into the house, so I drove the length of the Judengasse and half through the town, returned to the station and then to the Judengasse, and this time I stopped.

I said nothing as I helped her out of the car holding her large hand and feeling her elbow in my left palm once more. I took the suitcase, went to the front door, rang the bell and looked round at her as she followed, carrying her handbag. I ran up the steps with the case, put it outside the door, and met her as she slowly came up the steps carrying her handbag. I did not know how to address her, for neither Hedwig nor Fräulein Muller seemed to suit her, so I said: "I'll be back in half an hour to take you to lunch. All right?"

She merely nodded and stared past me, thoughtfully as though she were swallowing something. I said no more, ran back to my car and drove off into the blue. I do not know through which streets I drove nor what I thought, I only knew that the car was terribly empty, the car in which I was nearly always alone except occasionally with Ulla, and I tried to picture how it had been an hour ago, when I drove without her to the station.

But I could not remember what had gone before; I saw myself alone in the car driving to the station, as one might see a twin brother who is your perfect double, but with whom you actually have nothing in common. I came to my senses as I approached a florist's. I stopped and went into the shop. It was cool inside and smelt of flowers, and I was alone. There must be green roses, I thought, roses with green blossoms, and I caught sight of myself in the mirror taking money out of my wallet. I did not immediately recognise myself in the mirror and blushed because I had thought aloud, "Green roses," and felt that I was being watched. I only recognised myself by the flush which rose to my cheeks, and thought: So that's you; you really look very well bred. An old woman came from the back of the shop and in the distance I could see her false teeth gleaming as she smiled. She swallowed a mouthful of her lunch and the smile reappeared, and yet I thought she had merely swallowed her smile. I saw by her face that she had summed me up as a red-roses customer; with a smile she went over to a huge bunch of red roses standing in a silver vase; stroked one of the blooms with her finger. The gesture appeared to me obscene; it reminded me of the brothel against which Herr Brotig, my landlady's husband, had warned me. Suddenly I knew why I felt so uncomfortable; it was like being in a brothel; I knew it, although I had never actually been in one.

"They're lovely, aren't they?" said the woman. But I did not want the red roses, I had never liked them. "White," I said hoarsely, and she went with a smile to a bronze vase full of white roses. "Ah, for a wedding!"

"Yes," I replied, "for a wedding."

I had two notes and some loose change in my coat pocket. I piled it all on the counter. As I had once as a child laid pennies on the counter and said, "Give me sweets for that," I now said: "Give me white roses for the money . . . with a lot of green."

The woman took the money gingerly, counted it, and calculated on a piece of white paper how many roses I could buy. She did not smile now that she was working out the figure, but as she went over to the bronze vase with the white roses the smile suddenly reappeared. She had brought it up again. The overpowering scent in the air suddenly intoxicated me like a deadly poison; I went over to the counter, grabbed my money and ran out of the shop.

I jumped into my car—I saw myself from a great distance jumping into the car like someone who has robbed the till—and drove away and when I arrived at the station it struck me that I had seen it a thousand times a day for centuries and yet the station clock stood at ten minutes past twelve and it had been a quarter to twelve when I had put my penny in the platform ticket machine. I still seemed to hear the whirl of the groschen being caught in the cogs and the slight click when the cardboard ticket was ejected, and yet in the meantime I had forgotten who I was, what I looked like, and what I was by profession.

I drove round the station, stopped at the flower stall outside the Artisans' Bank, got out and bought three marks' worth of yellow tulips; there were ten and I handed the woman another three marks and was given another ten. I carried the flowers to the car, threw them into the back next to my tool-bag, walked past the flower booth and into the bank. When I took my cheque book from my inside pocket and walked slowly to the cashier's desk, I felt a trifle ridiculous and was afraid they would not pay me the money. I had written my balance on the green cover of the cheque book—1,710.80 marks—and as I slowly made out a cheque wrote "1,700:00" in the top right-hand corner and wrote "1,700 marks only" in words and signed the cheque with my name, Walter Fendrich, I felt like a forger. I was still afraid when I handed the cheque to the cashier's assistant, but she took it without so much as looking at me, put it in a bobbin and gave me a yellow cardboard number. I stood by the window, saw the cheques come back to the cashier in another bobbin; mine was among them, and I was surprised when he called out my number, and on handing him the cardboard slip over the white marble slab I was given the money. There were ten one-hundred-mark notes and fourteen fifties.

I found it remarkable that I had come out of the bank with money in my pocket. It was my own money, which I had saved, and it had not been difficult to save because I had earned good money, but the white marble pillars, the gilded door by which I left and the grave face of the porter made me feel that I had stolen my own money.

But as soon as I got into my car I laughed and drove quickly back to the Judengasse.

I rang Frau Grohlta's bell, pushed the door open with my back and climbed wearily up the stairs. I was desperately afraid of what was about to happen. I held the bunch of tulips head downwards in my hand, carrying it like a paper bag full of potatoes. I went straight upstairs without looking to right or left. I do not know what sort of grimace the landlady made as I passed, for I did not look at her.

Hedwig sat at the window with a book in her hand and I saw at once that she had not been reading. I had crept along the corridor to the door of her bedroom and had opened it noiselessly, as a thief would open a door (and yet I had never practised or learned the art). She closed her book abruptly, and this little gesture was as unforgettable as her smile. I can still hear the two halves of the book snapping to—the season ticket which she was using as a book-marker flew out and neither of us bent down to pick it up.

I remained standing by the door, looking at the old trees in the garden, at Hedwig's clothes which she had unpacked and laid untidily on the table and chair, and at the red-and-grey book she was reading—a Manual for Teachers. She now stood between the bed and the window with her arms dangling, her fists slightly clenched like someone who is about to beat a drum but has not yet picked up the sticks. I looked at her but I was not thinking of her. I was thinking of what Wickweber's assistant, with whom I had worked as a first-year apprentice, had told me. His name was Grommig. He was tall and lean and his forearm was covered with scars from hand-grenade splinters. During the war he had sometimes covered the faces of women he had possessed with a handkerchief, and I had been surprised how little shocked I had been at his descriptions.

The shock of his description only set in now as I stood facing Hedwig with the flowers in my hand—six years later, and what Grommig had told me seemed to me worse than anything else I could possibly have heard. The assistants had told me many hideous things, but none of them had covered the face of a woman with a handkerchief. And those who had not done so now appeared to me as innocent as children. Hedwig's face—I could hardly think of anything else.

"Leave me," she said. "Leave me at once."

"Yes," I replied. "I'm going." But I made no

move. I had never done with a woman what I wanted to do. There were many names for it, many words, and I knew nearly all of them. I had learned them during my apprentice days in the home and from my schoolmates at the engineering school. But none of these words described what I wanted to do with her, and I am still in search of that word. Love is not the word that expresses everything; perhaps only what comes nearest to the act itself.

I read on Hedwig's face what could be read in mine—fear and terror, not of what is called pleasure, but of all that which men had told me they had sought and never found. And I suddenly knew that not even Grommig was excluded. Behind the handkerchief which he threw over the face of the woman he had sought beauty. He need only, I felt, have removed the handkerchief in order to find it. What had been reflected in Hedwig's face slowly vanished from mine and her real face which had impressed me so deeply emerged again.

"You must go now," she said.

"Would you like the flowers?" I asked.

"Yes."

I laid them on her bed, wrapped up in their cellophane, watched her unpack them, straighten the buds and caress the green. She gave the impression that she received flowers every day.

"Pass me the vase, please," she said, and I handed her the vase which stood on the chest of drawers near the door. She came a few steps towards me, and as she took the vase from me I touched her hand for a second, and during that second I thought of everything I could have tried —to draw her towards me, to kiss her and never let her go. I made no attempt but stood with my back to the wall and watched her pour the water from the carafe into the vase and put the flowers in it. It was a dark red china vase and the flowers looked beautiful when she placed them in the window.

"Go now," she repeated, and I turned round without saying a word, opened the door and went out into the corridor. It was dark in this corridor because it had no window. A dark grey light filtered through the milky glass pane of the landing door. I wished that she had followed me and said something, but since she did not come I opened the landing door and went downstairs.

I stood in the entrance smoking a cigarette, looking at the sunny streets and reading the name-plates: Huhnert, Schmitz, Stephanides, Kroll—next came the name of her landlady, Grohlta, and a shop sign, Flink—Laundry; this was the launderette.

Before I had finished my cigarette I crossed

the street and stood on the other pavement watching the entrance. I gave a start when Frau Flink, the proprietress of the launderette, spoke to me. She must have crossed the street in her white overall, but I had not seen her.

"Ah, Herr Fendrich," she said, "you've come at the right moment. One of the machines is beginning to run hot. The girl has done something stupid."

"Disconnect it," I said, without looking at Frau Flink. I continued to stare at the entrance.

"Can't you have a look at it?"

"No, I can't."

"But you're on the spot here."

"Yes, I'm on the spot," I replied, "but I can't attend to the machine. I have to stand here."

"Well, I'm . . ." spluttered Frau Flink. "You're standing here and you can't even come and have a look at my machine?"

Out of the corner of my eye I saw Frau Flink cross the street and a moment later her work-girls—four or five white overalls—appeared at the door of the launderette. I heard them laughing, but I was quite indifferent.

It must be like this, I thought, when you drown. Grey water runs into you, a lot of water. You see no more, hear no more, only a dull roar and the grey brackish-tasting water seems sweet to you.

My brain went on working like a machine which someone had forgotten to turn off. I suddenly found the solution of an algebra problem which I had not been able to solve two years ago in my exam at the engineering school, and I was delighted that I had found the solution—the same delight you feel when you suddenly remember a name or a word which has slipped your memory. English words that I had not known at school nine years ago came into my head, and I suddenly knew that *Zundholz* was a match. Ted brought his father a match and Ted's father lit his pipe with this match. The fire burnt in the grate and Ted's father put on a new log before he began to tell the story of his days in India. *Scheit* meant a log, and now I could have translated the sentence which no one, not even in the Upper First, could have translated. It was as though someone in a dream whispered the words I had never read or heard. My eyes, however, held fast on to one picture—the front door through which Hedwig must eventually come. It was a newly painted brown front door and I felt that I had never seen anything else in the world except this door.

I do not know if I suffered. The dark grey waters flowed over me and yet I was more wide awake than I had ever been. I thought that some time later I must apologise to Frau Flink. She had always been nice to me and had found the room for Hedwig, and sometimes when I was tired she made me coffee. Some time later, I thought, I must apologise to her. There was a lot I had to do, and I thought of everything and also of the woman in the Kurbelstrasse who had wept on the telephone and was still waiting for me.

I knew now what I had always known but had refused to admit for six years—that I hated this profession as I had hated all the other professions I had ever tried. I loathed these washing machines, and the smell of soap flakes made me feel sick. A disgust that was more than physical. . . . What I loved about this profession was the money that it brought in and the money I had in my pocket. I felt for it—it was still there.

I smoked another cigarette, but that, too, I did mechanically—took the packet from my pocket, tapped the cigarette, and for a second saw the house door red through the little flame of the lighter, then wreathed in blue from the smoke of my cigarette, but I did not enjoy the cigarette and I threw it away, half smoked, into the gutter. When I wanted to light another one, I felt, by the weight of the packet, that it was empty. So I threw the packet, too, into the gutter.

The knowledge that I was hungry and that a slight nausea circled within me like liquid in a filter all took place outside me. I had never been able to sing, but here opposite the house door through which Hedwig would eventually come I could have sung—I knew it.

I had always known that Wickweber, although keeping within the law, was a cheat. But here, for the first time, on the rough basalt kerb opposite this house door, I worked out the formula of his roguery. I had worked for two years in his factory and later had to check and pass the utensils he made there—utensils whose sale price I calculated with Wickweber and Ulla. The material was cheap and it was good—as good as the material which had been used for U-boats and aircraft—and Wickweber received it by the truck-load, and we had calculated the sale price of a hot-water boiler at ninety marks. That was the price one paid for three loaves when the market, as they termed it, was saturated. And it was the price of two loaves when the market, as they termed it, was in short supply. I had tried out the boiler in the cabin above the wages office and stamped my "F" and the date before the apprentice took it down to the store-room to be packed in greaseproof paper. And a year ago I bought a boiler for Father which Wickweber let me have at cost price. And the foreman had taken me into the store-room and let me choose one. I packed it in my car, delivered it to Father, and when I assembled it I discovered my own "F" and the date 19.2.47. And I found it remarkable and had given it some thought, as one thinks of an equation in which there is one unknown quantity. And on the kerb now in front of Hedwig's door it was no longer remarkable and I knew the unknown quantity. What in those days had cost three loaves was now sold for the price of two hundred loaves, and I myself, who received a percentage, still paid as much for it as a hundred and thirty loaves cost, and I was surprised that it was so much, that the unknown quantity represented such a value. And I thought of all the electric irons, boilers, electric heaters and ovens on which I had stamped my "F" during the past two years.

I thought of the rage I had felt as a boy when I spent the winter with my parents in the Alps. Father had photographed Mother against the snow-covered peaks. She had black hair and wore a light coat. I had stood beside him when he took the picture. Everything was white except Mother's black hair. But when Father showed me the negative at home it looked as though a white-haired negress was standing in front of a huge slag-heap. I was furious, and the comparatively simple scientific explanation did not satisfy me. I had always felt until this moment that it could not be explained by a few chemical formulae with solutions and salts. On the other hand, the words "dark room" had intoxicated me—and later, to pacify me, Father photographed Mother in a black coat in front of a slag-heap in our town. Then on the negative I saw a white-haired negress in a white coat standing in front of tall snowy mountains. The only dark thing now was what had been light in Mother—her white face. But her black coat and the slag-heap looked light and gay as though Mother stood smiling in the snow.

My anger was just as bitter at this second snapshot, and since then photographic prints have never interested me. I have always thought that no prints should be made of photos, for that was the least interesting thing about them. I wanted to see the negative, and I was fascinated by the dark room where in a red light Father let the negatives swim for a long time in mysterious dishes until snow became snow and coal coal. But it was bad snow and bad coal . . . and it seemed to me that the snow in the negative had been good coal and the coal in the negative good snow. Father had tried to console me by saying that there was only one true print of everything, and this lay in a dark room we did not know—in the memory of God. But this explanation at the time had sounded too simple because God was merely a great word with which grown-ups tried to cover up everything.

But here, standing on the kerb, I felt that I understood Father. I knew that I should be photographed just as I stood there. There was a picture of me as I stood there—so deep below the surface of the grey waters—there was a picture of me and I longed to see it. Had someone spoken English to me I could have replied to him in English. And here on the kerb in front of Hedwig's house was revealed to me that what I had always been too afraid to admit, what I had always been too shy to say meant a great deal to me—to arrive at evening Mass before the sacrifice, and even more to remain seated there, while the church was emptying, often until the sexton ostentatiously rattled his bunch of keys just as waiters will ostentatiously pile the chairs up on the tables when they want to leave, and the grief at having to leave the tavern is not unlike the grief I felt when I was turned out of the church which I had entered at the very last moment. I also seemed to understand now what I had hitherto been incapable of understanding: that Wickweber could be pious and yet a rogue, and that he was genuine in both. Pious and rascally, and I surrendered my hatred for him as a child with a toy balloon which he has clutched a whole summer Sunday afternoon suddenly releases it to see it rise into the evening sky, until it grows smaller and smaller and is no longer visible. I could hear my light sigh as I suddenly released my hatred for Wickweber.

"Fly away," I thought, and for a moment I took my eyes from the door and tried to follow my sigh. And for that moment where my hatred had been remained an empty space, a very slight emptiness which seemed to carry me as the gills carry a fish—only for a moment, and then I felt that this space had been filled with something as heavy as lead—with mortal indifference. From time to time I looked at my wrist-watch but never at the hour or the minute hand, only at the little circle above the six. There alone time passed for me, and only this thin rapid finger below moved me, not the large slow ones up there, and this swift thin finger ran very fast—a small precision machine which cut discs of something invisible from time, and bored into nothingness, and the dust that it bored out of nothingness fell on me like an enchanted powder, transforming me into a motionless pillar.

I saw the girls leave the launderette at midday and saw them return. I saw Frau Flink standing in the doorway of her shop, shaking her head. People passed behind me, people passed the house door from which Hedwig eventually had to come; people that masked the door for a moment, and I thought of everything I should by rights have done. The names of five customers stood on a white slip in my car, and at six o'clock I had an appointment with Ulla in the Café Joos, but I always dismissed Ulla from my mind.

It was Monday, the 14th of March, and Hedwig did not appear. I held the wrist-watch to my left ear and heard the mocking industry of the little hand, boring holes in the void, dark circular holes that began to dance before my eyes, grouped themselves round the house door, dissolved once more and disappeared in the pale sky like coins thrown into the water. Then once more my field of vision was pierced like the sheet of metal from which I had cut square nickel discs in Wickweber's factory. And in each of these holes I saw the door, saw it a hundred times, always the same door—tiny but very accurate house doors attached in the thin perforations like stamps on a large sheet; a hundred times the face of the inventor of the sparking plug.

I felt aimlessly in my pocket for cigarettes although I knew that I had none left. There was another packet in the car, but the car was twenty yards to the right of the door and a whole ocean lay between me and the car. And I thought once more of the woman in the Kurbelstrasse who had wept on the telephone as only women weep who cannot cope with their husbands. And I suddenly knew that it was pointless dismissing Ulla from my mind and I thought of her. I did it as one suddenly decides to switch on the light in a room where someone has died. The half light has made the corpse look like a person asleep and one imagines that one can hear him breathe and see his movements. But now the light falls harshly on the scene and one sees the preparations for the funeral have already taken place. The candelabra stand there, the pots of palms, and somewhere to the left beneath the dead man's feet is a hump where the black cloth bellies ominously. The man from the undertakers has already left the hammer with which tomorrow he will nail down the coffin lid. And one can already hear what will not be heard until tomorrow, the irrevocable naked hammer that has no melody.

The fact that Ulla still knew nothing made thinking about her even more difficult. Nothing could be changed, the clock would not be put back any more than the nails could be removed from the coffin lid. But she was still in ignorance.

I thought of the life that I should have led with her. She had always watched me as you watch a hand grenade which has been made into an ash-tray to stand on the piano. You shake your ash into it on Sunday after coffee, you clean it on Monday, and while you clean it you still have the same tantalising feeling at seeing a once so dangerous object being used in such a harmless way. The wit who made the ashtray has used the pin in an original manner—you can pull the white china button which looks like the china button of a bedside lamp and a hidden battery kindles a few wires at which you can light your cigarette. Today it is a peaceful object which had been devised for such unpeaceful ends. Nine hundred and ninety times you can pull the pin without causing any damage, and yet no one knows that at the thousandth time a hidden mechanism will be put in motion to make the witty toy explode. Nothing terrible happens. A few bits of iron shrapnel which will not hit you in the heart. They give you a fright and you pay more attention in future.

Nothing terrible would happen to Ulla and her heart would not be touched, but she would be wounded everywhere except in the heart. She would talk, talk a great deal, and I knew exactly what she would say. By and large she would be in the right, and would wish to be in the right, and she would gloat a little, and I had always hated people who were right and gloated when it turned out that they were really in the right. They had always appeared to me like people who take a newspaper but always overlook that somewhere in the edition is a trace of a higher power—and then display righteous indignation when one morning the paper does not appear. As in life insurance policies, they should have read the small print more carefully than the headlines.

Only when I could no longer see the door did I realise for whom I was waiting—for Hedwig. I could no longer see the door. It was masked by a large dark red truck which I knew only too well; "Wickweber's Sanitary Service" was painted on the car in cream-coloured letters, and I crossed the street because I had to keep my eye on the door. I advanced slowly, like a man swimming under water, and I sighed as a man might sigh who is swimming through forests of seaweed and oyster-beds, past terrified fish slowly along the steep bank which has assumed the proportions of a mountain and is appalled because he no longer feels the weight of the water pressure on his neck but the lightness of the air pressure which we accept too casually.

I walked round the truck, and when I saw the door again I knew that Hedwig would not come down. She lay up there on her bed covered with invisible dust that the second hand had bored out of the void.

I was pleased that she had sent me away when I arrived with the flowers. I was pleased that she had known at once what I wanted to do with her and I was afraid of the moment when she would no longer send me away—a moment that would come some time today, which was still Monday.

The house door was now a matter of indifference, and I considered myself foolish, almost as foolish as in the old days when I had secretly kissed my landlady's apron. I went over to my car, opened the door, took out the packet of cigarettes which lay in the right-hand pocket under my receipt book for fares and working hours. I lit a cigarette, closed the door and did not know what to do—whether to go up to Hedwig's room or to drive to the woman in the Kurbelstrasse who had wept so bitterly on the telephone.

Suddenly Wolf's hand lay on my shoulder. I felt it as I had felt the weight of the water pressure, and out of my left eye I could even see the hand. It was a hand that had offered me countless cigarettes and had accepted as many from me—a clean, capable hand, and I could even see the sparkle of his engagement ring in the March sun. I could feel by its slight tremor that Wolf was laughing—that light, gurgling laughter when he had laughed in the engineering school at the jokes of our teacher. And in the second before I turned round to him I recalled what I had felt when Father had persuaded me to attend a reunion of former schoolmates. I saw myself sitting there with boys whose lives I had shared for three, four, six or nine years, boys with whom I had cowered in air-raid shelters while the bombs fell. Our studies in class were the battles we had fought side by side. We had put out the fire in the burning school, bandaged the wounded Latin master and carried him to safety. We had been ploughed together, and it seemed as though these experiences would bind us together for ever but they had proved no bond. Far from being an eternal bond, my only memories were the insipid taste of the first secretly smoked cigarette and a desire to put my hand on the arm of the waitress who brought the beer—the girl you see for the first time in your life who suddenly becomes an old acquaintance, almost as much trusted as your mother. . . . Compared with the hostility you feel for those whose wisdom resides in the fact that they have lost ideals they never had, ideals you began to love because you had lost them—unhappy oafs who all turn away when you ask them how much a month they earn. You suddenly know that the only friend you had was the boy in the Second who died: Jurgen Brolaski. The boy with whom you never exchanged a word because he had seemed unsympathetic and fusty. Drowned out swimming one summer evening, caught under a raft down by the sawmill where the willows had sprouted through the blue basalt of the quay wall, where one could roller skate in bathing costume down the concrete slipways, where the trunks were high—on roller skates down to the water. Weeds between the paving stones and the pathetic "That's enough now. That's enough" of the night watchman, collecting firewood for his stove. Brolaski with his skinny body who had no roller skates and wore a pink bathing costume which his mother had cut out from a petticoat. Sometimes I thought that he stayed in the water so that we should not see his bathing trunks. Occasionally he climbed on to the raft, sat down with his arms in his lap, gazing out over the Rhine, peering into the dark green shadows of the bridge which in the evening stretched as far as the sawmill. No one saw him jump into the water. No one missed him until his mother ran weeping through the streets that night from house to house crying: "Have you seen my boy? Haven't you seen Jurgen?" "No . . ."

Brolaski's father stood in uniform by the grave, a corporal with no decorations. He raised his head pensively as we sang: "Early to the grave, Brother. Death has called thee early to the grave . . . early to the grave."

During the class reunion I could only think of Brolaski and the beautiful white arm of the waitress on which I should have so much liked to lay my hand. Brolaski's pale pink bathing trunks cut from his mother's petticoat, with a broad elastic band to keep them up. Brolaski who had vanished in the dark green shadows of the bridge. . . .

"Brother—death has called thee early to the grave. . . ."

I turned round slowly to Wolf and looked at his good, capable face which I had known for seven years. I felt a little ashamed, as I had once felt when Father caught me stealing a stamped good conduct certificate.

"You must help me," said Wolf. "I can't find the fault. Please come."

He took me gently by the hand as one leads a blind man and led me slowly over to the launderette. I smelled what I smelled so often every day—the stench of dirty washing; I saw piles of it lying there and I saw Frau Flink and the girls standing in their overalls as one sees in the cloud of dust after an explosion people one had expected to be dead.

"It runs hot," I heard. "I've tried it three times. . . . No good. All the machines—all of them."

"Did you unscrew the filters?" I asked Wolf.

"Yes—they were dirty. I've cleaned them. Did it a second time and all the machines still ran hot."

"I'm losing my best client," said Frau Flink. "The Hunnenhof proprietor is my best client and

I shall lose him if his bedding isn't there tonight."

"Unscrew the water pipe," I said to Wolf, and I saw him unscrew the leads to all four machines. And at the same time I heard the girls discussing the bed linen and the gossip they learned from the hotel chambermaids. They had often shown me triumphantly the sheets of Ministers stained with actresses' lipstick, held them up to me so that I could smell the expensive perfume the mistress of some party official used. Previously these things had amused me, but I suddenly realised how indifferent I was to Ministers and party officials. Not even their private lives interested me. The secrets of their private lives could vanish with the detergent which ran out of the machine. I wanted to get outside. I hated the machines and loathed the stench of soap flakes.

With a giggle the girls handed round the sheets of a film star whose perversions were well known.

Wolf had unscrewed all the water pipes and looked at me. He looked a trifle stupid.

"Has the town water system been repaired?" I asked Frau Flink without looking at her.

"Yes," she said. "They pulled up the Korbmachergrasse yesterday from where our water comes."

"Yes," said Wolf, who had let the water run. "It's rusty and dirty."

"Let it run until it comes through clear, then screw up the pipes and it will be all right."

"You won't lose your best client," I said to Frau Flink; "the washing will be ready by this evening," and I went out into the street as one goes from one landscape to another in a dream.

I sat on the running board of Wickweber's truck but I did not stare at the house door. I closed my eyes and for a moment saw the dark room and the picture of the only man I knew who had never shouted or roared at another man, the only man of whose piety I was convinced. I saw Father. In front of him stood the card index, a blue wooden box in which we kept our dominoes in the old days. It was always crammed full with slips of the same size which Father cut out of old papers. Hoarding paper was his only avarice. From letters begun and thrown away, from partially filled school notebooks he tore out the empty pages; he cut off the unprinted parts of marriage and funeral cards and from those ceremonious hand-made paper exhortations to attend some manifestation, linen invitation cards which had something to do with the cause of freedom. This printed matter filled him with a childish glee because from each he could get at least six filing cards to be preserved like treasures in the old domino box. He was a card index man. He stuck the cards in his books;

his briefcase was full of them. He entrusted important and unimportant matters to these cards. I often found some when I was at home. "The button on my pants" stood on one, on a second "Mozart," and on another "pilageuse—pilage." Once I found one which read: "I saw a face in the tram which Jesus Christ must have worn at Gethsemane." Before he went shopping he took out his slips, ran through them as one runs through a pack of cards, spread them out like a game of patience and arranged them according to their importance in little piles as though separating aces, kings, queens and jacks.

They protruded from the pages of all his books; most of them were dog-eared, or spotted yellow, because he often let the books lie around for months before dealing with the card. During the school holidays he collected them, re-read the passages to which the notes referred, collated the English and French words, phrase constructions and usages whose meaning only became clear when two or three of them corresponded. He conducted a vast correspondence about his discoveries, sent for lexicons, checked with his colleagues, and with amiable tenacity pestered the publishers of works on philology.

He always carried one particular card in his briefcase; it was underlined with red pencil as being very important—a card he destroyed after each of my visits but soon rewrote—the card on which was written: "Talk to the boy!"

I remembered how surprised I had been to discover the same obstinacy in myself during the years I attended the engineers' school. What I knew and what I realised never excited me as much as what I did not know and could not realise. I knew no peace until I could dismantle and assemble a new machine almost in my sleep. My curiosity, however, always went hand in hand with the desire to turn my knowledge into money—a motive that Father never understood. What a single word often cost in postage, when books were sent to and fro and journeys had to be made, did not count for him. He loved these newly discovered words or usages as a zoologist loves a newly discovered animal, and he would never have dreamed of taking money for his discoveries.

. . . . .

Wolf's hand lay once more on my shoulder, and I realised that I had got off the running board, gone over to my own car and was looking through the windscreen at the place where Hedwig had sat. It was empty....

"What's the matter?" asked Wolf. "What have you done to poor Frau Flink? She's quite upset."

I did not reply. Wolf kept his hand on my shoulder, pushed me past my car into the Korbmachergasse. "She telephoned me," he said, "and there was something in her voice which made me come at once. . . . Something which had nothing to do with her machines."

I remained silent. "Come," said Wolf. "A coffee will do you good."

"Yes," I replied gently. "A coffee will do me good." I freed my shoulder and went on ahead of him along the Korbmachergasse, where I knew a little café.

A young woman was already shaking rolls out of a white linen sack into the window. The rolls were piled in front of the pane and I could see their smooth brown bellies, their crisp backs and the white, very white tops where the baker had cut the dough. They continued to slip after the young woman had returned to the shop, and for a moment they reminded me of silly flatfish in an aquarium.

"Here?" asked Wolf.

"Yes, here."

He shook his head but smiled when I walked past the counter into the little empty back room. "Not so bad," he said as he sat down.

"No, not at all bad."

"Oh," said Wolf, "one's only got to look at you to know what's up."

"What is up, then?" I asked.

"Oh, nothing," he grinned "You merely look like someone who has decided to commit suicide. I see that I can't count on you any more today."

The girl brought the coffee which Wolf had ordered in the front shop.

"Father's livid," he said. "The telephone's been going all day and you couldn't be found. You couldn't even be reached under the number you left with Frau Brotig. Don't get his back up too much. He's very angry. You know he never jokes when it's a question of business."

I drank my coffee, stood up, went into the shop and ordered three rolls from the girl. She gave me a plate, but I shook my head when she offered me a knife. I put the rolls on the plate, returned to the back shop, sat down and ripped one of them open by sticking both thumbs in the white cut and then breaking it outwards. As soon as I had eaten the first mouthful I felt that the nausea had vanished in my belly.

"My God," said Wolf. "You don't need to eat dry bread."

"No—I don't need to."

"One just can't talk to you today," he said.

"No—one can't talk to me today. You'd better go."

"All right," he said. "Perhaps you'll be normal again tomorrow."

He stood up with a laugh, called the woman from the shop, paid for the two cups of coffee and three rolls, and when he added two groschen as a tip the girl smiled and put the coins back in his clean capable hand. With a shake of his head he put them back in his purse. As I opened the two rolls I felt Wolf's eyes on the back of my neck, run over my hair and down my face to my hands.

"By the way," he said, "it came off."

I looked at him questioningly.

"Didn't Ulla tell you yesterday about the contract for Tritonia?"

"Yes," I replied casually. "She told me about it yesterday."

"We've got the contract," said Wolf with a broad smile. "This morning the adjudication was granted. I hope you'll be ready to start costing when we start on Friday. What on earth can I say to Father? He's angrier with you than he's been since that silly business in the old days."

I laid aside my roll and stood up.

"Since what business?" I asked. I saw by his face that he regretted having mentioned it. But he had mentioned it, and I opened my back trouser pocket in which my money lay, ran the notes through my hand and suddenly realised that they were only hundreds and fifties. I rebuttoned my back pocket and felt in my overcoat for the change I had been given at the flower stall. I took Wolf's right hand, opened it and pressed a twenty-mark note, a two-mark piece and fifty pfennigs into his palm.

"That's for the business in the old days," I said. "The oven tops I pinched cost two marks fifty-five. Give your Father the money. There were ten of them. That was six years ago, but you hadn't forgotten. I'm glad you reminded me."

"I'm sorry I mentioned it," said Wolf.

"You mentioned it here and now. Now you've got the money, give it to your father."

"Take the money back," he said. "You can't do that."

"Why not?" I replied calmly. "I stole them at the time and now I'm paying for what I stole. Anything else on the bill?"

He fell silent, and now I was sorry for him because he did not know what to do with the money. He held it in his hand and I saw the drops of sweat in his clenched hand and on his face, and he made the same face as when the assistants swore at him or told dirty stories.

"We were both sixteen when it happened," I said. "We started our apprenticeship together. But you're twenty-three now and you've never forgotten it. Come, give me the money back if it torments you. I can always send it to your father."

I opened his hand again. It was warm and sweaty and I put the coins and the note back in my overcoat pocket.

"Go now," I said gently. But he stood there and looked at me as he had once looked at me when it was discovered that I had stolen. He had not believed it and had defended me in his clear, eager boyish voice. And I felt at the time, although we were exactly the same age, that he was like a much younger brother who takes the thrashing the other has deserved. The old man had roared at him and slapped his face and I would have given a thousand loaves if I could have denied the theft. But I had to admit it—outside in the courtyard in front of the gloomy workshop lit by the pitiful fifteen-watt bulbs which hung in rusty fixtures and wobbled in the November wind. Wolf's clear childish protesting voice had been killed by my pathetic "Yes" when the old man asked me the direct question. They had gone together across the courtyard into their house. Wolf had always taken me for what, in his childish heart, he considered "a fine chap." And it was painful for me to forfeit this title. I felt stupid and miserable when I returned by tram to the apprentices' home. I had not the slightest prick of conscience for having pinched the oven tops, which I had exchanged for bread and cigarettes. I had already begun to have some thoughts about prices. It did not matter to me that Wolf took me for "a fine chap," but it mattered that for no just reason he did not continue to think me one.

The following morning the old man called me into his office and sent Veronica outside. His swarthy hands toyed nervously with his cigar. Then he took off his green felt hat—a thing he never did—and said: "I've just telephoned to Chaplain Derichs and learned that your mother died recently. We'll never mention it again, never, do you hear? Now go."

I went, and when I returned to the workshop I thought: "Never mention what?" Mother's death? And I hated the old man more bitterly than ever. I did not know the reason but I knew that I had good reason. Since then the subject was never mentioned again, never. And I had never stolen again, never. Not because I considered theft unjustifiable but because it was terrible to be forgiven something because one's mother had died.

"Go now," I said to Wolf. Go. . . ."

"I'm sorry," he said. "It . . . I . . ." His eyes looked as though he still believed in fine chaps, and I said: "It's all right. Don't think about it any more, but go."

He now looked as men of forty look when they

lose what they call their ideals—a little flabby and friendly and even perhaps what they call a fine chap.

"What shall I say to Father?"

"Did he send you?"

"No, but I only know that he's very angry, and that he'll try to get in touch with you to discuss the Tritonia contract."

"I don't know yet what will happen."

"Don't you really know?"

"No, really not."

"Is it right what Frau Flink's girls said? That you're chasing a girl?"

"Yes. They're quite right. I'm chasing a girl."

"My God," said Wolf. "I shouldn't leave you alone with all that money in your pocket."

"But you must," I said quietly. "Go now; and please," I lowered my voice, "don't ask me what you have to say to your father."

He left, and I saw him pass the shop window with his arms dangling like a boxer about to enter the ring for a hopeless fight. I waited until he had disappeared round the corner of the Korbmachergasse, then I took up my position in the open shop door and waited until I saw Wickweber's truck drive off in the direction of the station. I returned to the back room, drank the coffee standing up and stuffed a third roll in my pocket. I looked at my wrist-watch where the hands were moving forward slowly and noiselessly, and I hoped that it would be half-past five or six but it was only four. I said *Auf wiedersehen* to the young woman behind the counter and returned to my car. In the cleft between the two seats I saw the end of the white slip on which that morning I had written the names of the clients I had to visit. I opened the car door, rescued the slip, tore it up and threw the fragments into the gutter.

I should have preferred to return to the other side of the street and to have sunk, deep, very deep below the waves, but I blushed at the very thought of it, went over to the front door of the house in which Hedwig lived and rang the bell. I rang twice, three times and once more, and waited for the noise of the buzzer, but it did not come, so I pressed twice more on the bell and I was afraid—the same fear I had felt before I joined Hedwig on the other side of the platform steps. But then I heard footsteps—footsteps which could not belong to Frau Grohlta—rapid footsteps coming down the stairs and along the corridor and Hedwig opened the door. She was taller than I had thought and we both drew back as we suddenly stood so close to each other. She stepped back a pace but held the door open and I knew how heavy the door was, because we had to hold it open when we carried in the machines for Frau Flink, until the laundress had fastened the door back on its hook.

"There's a hook on the door," I said.

"Where?" asked Hedwig.

"Here," I replied, knocking above the door-knob from outside; her left hand and face disappeared for a few seconds in the darkness behind the door. The light from the street gave me a close view of her. I knew that it was terrible for her to be stared at like this, as a picture is stared at. She did not avert her eyes but let her lower lip drop a little and returned my stare and I felt my fear vanish, felt once more the anguish this face caused.

"In the old days," I said, "you were fair-haired'.'

"How long ago?" she asked.

"Seven years, just before I left home."

"Yes," she said with a smile, "in those days I was fair-haired and anaemic."

"I looked for a blonde girl this morning," I said, "and there you were sitting behind me the whole time on your suitcase."

"Not long," she replied. "I had just sat down when you came. I recognised you at once but I didn't want to speak to you." She smiled once more.

"Why?" I asked.

"Because you looked so angry, and because you looked so grown up and important. I'm always scared of important people."

"What did you think?" I asked.

"Oh, nothing. I thought: So that's the young Fendrich. You look much younger in the photograph your father has of you. They don't say nice things about you. Someone told me you were a thief." She turned red and I could see for myself that she was no longer anaemic; she was so fiery red that I could not bear to see it.

"No," I said gently, "you needn't blush. I did really steal, but that was six years ago, and if things were the same I should do it again. Who told you?"

"My brother, and he is not a bad fellow."

"No," I repeated, "he is not a bad fellow. And you thought that I was a thief because I went away?"

"Yes, I thought so, but not for long."

"How long?" I asked.

"I don't know," she said with a smile. "I also thought of other things. I was hungry but I was afraid to come downstairs because I knew that you were standing here."

I took the roll out of my coat pocket. She took it with a smile and broke it and I saw her strong white thumbs sink into the soft dough as into a cushion. She took a bite and before she took the second I said: "Do you know who told your brother that I was a thief?"

"Does it mean such a lot to you to know?"

"Yes, a great deal."

"It must have been the people whom you—" she blushed again—"whom you robbed. My brother said: 'I have it on good authority.'" She ate her second mouthful, looked past me and said softly: "I'm sorry I sent you away like that, but I was afraid. But when I did it, I wasn't thinking of the story my brother told me."

"I almost wish," I said, "that I really had stolen, but the stupid thing is that it was only a clumsiness; I was too young at the time and too afraid. Today I would do it better."

"So you haven't a trace of regret?" she asked, eating another mouthful of the bread.

"No," I replied, "not the slightest—it was odious the way I did it, but I couldn't help it. And you forgive me—do you know how wonderful it is to be forgiven something which one does not consider to be a crime?"

"No, I don't know, but I think it's bad. Have you by any chance some more bread in your pocket?" she said with a smile. "What do you do with it? Do you feed the birds or are you afraid of hunger?"

"I'm always afraid of hunger," I replied. "Do you want some more bread?"

"Yes."

"Come, then," I said. "I'll buy you some."

"You'd think we were in the desert," she replied. "I haven't eaten or drunk for seven hours."

"Come."

She fell silent and was no longer smiling. "I'll come with you," she said slowly, "if you promise never to appear so abruptly and with so many flowers in my room."

"I promise you," I said.

She bent down behind the door and raised the hook and I heard it beat against the wall.

"It's not far," I said, "only round the corner. Come." But she stood there and kept the door opened with her back and waited for me to go ahead. I walked a little in front of her, and when I turned round I saw that she had brought her handbag with her.

Behind the counter in the café now stood a man with a big knife cutting fresh apple flans into slices, the brown trellis-work of dough above the green apple mousse was fresh and the man pressed the knife carefully into the cake so as not to destroy the pastry. We stood in silence at the counter watching him.

"They also have chicken soup and goulash here," I said to Hedwig.

"Yes," said the man, without looking up. "You can have some." His hair was black and thick where it protruded from his baker's cap, and the man smelt of bread as peasant girls smell of milk.

"No," said Hedwig. "No soup. Cakes."

"How many?" asked the man. He cut the last slice, pulled out the knife and looked at his work with satisfaction.

"Do you want to bet," he said, and his face wrinkled into a smile, "do you want to bet that the slices are exactly the same size and of the same weight?" He put down his knife. "At the utmost a difference of two or three grammes; that's unavoidable. Shall we bet?"

"No," I said with a smile. "I won't bet, because I should lose." The cakes looked like a rose window in a cathedral. "Yes, you'd certainly lose," said the man. "How many do you want?"

I looked at Hedwig questioningly. "One is too little and two are too many," she said with a smile.

"One and a half, then," said the man.

"Can I have that?" asked Hedwig.

"Of course," he replied, taking his knife and cutting one of the slices of pastry right through the middle. "One and a half each, and coffee."

The cups still stood on the table where I had sat with Wolf, and there were still crumbs of bread on my plate. Hedwig sat down on the stool on which Wolf had sat; I took out my packet of cigarettes and offered it to her. "No, thank you," she said. "Later, perhaps."

"I must ask you something," I said as I sat down. "Something I should have liked to ask your father, but I was naturally too scared."

"What is it?" she asked.

"How is it that you're called Muller and not Müller?"

"Ah! That's a silly business and it's often annoyed me."

"How do you mean?"

"My grandfather was called Müller. He was very rich and his name was too commonplace, so he paid an enormous sum of money to have the diaeresis removed. I'm furious with him."

"Why?"

"Because I like to be called Müller, and should have had the money that it cost to remove those silly little dots. I wish I had that money, for then I shouldn't have to be a teacher."

"Don't you want to be?" I asked.

"Oh, I don't mind, but I'm not crazy about it. Father said I had to be so that I can keep myself."

"If you like," I said gently, "I will keep you."

She blushed, and I was glad that I had said it at last and could say it in this way. I was also pleased that the man came at that moment with the coffee. He placed the pot on the table, removed the dirty crockery and said: "Do you want cream on your cakes?"

"Yes," I said, "I'd like some cream."

He left the room and Hedwig poured out the coffee. Her cheeks were still red and I stared over her head at the picture hanging on the wall. It was a photograph of a marble statue of a woman; I had often passed the statue and never knew whom it represented, and I was glad to be able to read now under the photograph, "Empress Augusta Memorial," and to learn who the woman was.

The man brought the cakes; I put milk in my coffee, stirred it, broke off a piece of cake with a spoon, and I was glad when Hedwig began to eat. She was no longer red, and said without looking up from her plate: "Strange diet—a lot of flowers eaten between two fires."

"And later," I added, "cream cakes and coffee, but at night what my mother used to call a proper dinner."

"Yes," she said, "my mother also used to say I should eat a proper meal every day."

"About seven, perhaps?"

"Today?" she asked.

"Yes."

"No," she replied. "I can't this evening. I have

to go and visit one of Father's relatives. She lives in a suburb and has been looking forward to my arrival."

"Don't you want to go?" I asked.

"No," she said. "She's one of those women who notice at the first glance when you've last washed the curtains, and the worst of it is what she says is always right. If she saw us here she'd say: 'He'll seduce you.' "

"That's right," I replied. "I want to seduce you."

"I know," said Hedwig. "No, I don't want to go and see her."

"Well, don't go," I advised. "It would be wonderful if I could see you again this evening. One shouldn't go and visit people one doesn't like."

"All right, I won't go, but if I don't she'll come and fetch me. She has a car and she's terribly efficient—no, resolute, Father always calls her."

"I hate resolute people," I said.

"So do I." She ate the rest of the cake, and scooped up the cream which had trickled out of the pastry with her spoon.

"I can't make up my mind to go where I have to go at six," I said. "I wanted to meet the girl I once wanted to marry, and to tell her that I won't marry her." She had picked up the coffee-pot to pour out a second cup, but now she held it in the air and asked: "Does it depend upon me if you tell her today or not?"

"No, it's my affair, but I must tell her in any case."

"Then go and tell her. Who is she?"

"The girl whose father I stole from, and also the one who repeated it and told your brother."

"Oh, well, that makes it quite easy."

"Too easy," I said. "Far too easy. It's almost like cancelling your newspaper, which not only harms the newspaper but the newspaper woman, who has a monthly tip less."

"Go and see her," said Hedwig, "and I won't go to Father's relative. When do you have to leave?"

"About six," I said. "But it's not yet five."

"You can leave me now," said Hedwig. "Find a stationer's and buy me a postcard. I promised I would write home every day."

"Would you like another coffee?" I asked.

"No, but you can give me a cigarette."

I handed her the packet and she took a cigarette. I lit it for her, and as I stood in the shop and paid I saw her sitting there smoking it. I could see that she seldom smoked by the way she held the cigarette and puffed out the smoke, and when I went back to her she looked up and said, "You must go now," and I left, and when I saw her open her handbag the lining was as green as her coat.

I went all along the Korbmachergasse, and turned at the corner into the Netzmachergasse; it had turned cool and the lights were already on in some of the shop windows. I had to go the whole length of the Netzmachergasse before I found a stationer's.

In the shop on old-fashioned shelves everything lay jumbled on top of each other. On the counter stood a pack of cards which someone had obviously opened and not found suitable, and the damaged cards lay next to the torn wrapper—an ace of diamonds, and the big diamond in the centre had faded, a torn nine of spades. A ball-point pen lay next to the block on which someone had tried it out. I rested my arm on the counter and examined the block—flourishes, stupid doodlings, and someone had written "Brunostrasse," but most people had practised their signature, and in the first letter one could see the jerk they had given to the pen. Maria Kahlisch, I read clearly in a firm round script, and someone else had written as a stammerer speaks, "Robert B—Robert Br—Robert Brach," and the handwriting was spidery, old-fashioned and pathetic, and I thought it must have been an old man's. Someone had written "Heinrich" and in the same handwriting "forget-me-not" and another with a thick nib had written *Bruchbude*.

At last a young woman appeared. She nodded

amiably to me and put the pack of cards with the two damaged cards back in the packet.

I asked to see some picture postcards, five different ones. I took them from the pile she laid in front of me, the top five. They were pictures of parks and churches and a picture of a statue I had not yet seen; it was called the Noldewohl Memorial, and showed a bronze man in a frock coat carrying a roll of paper which he had just opened.

"Who was Noldewohl?" I asked the woman, handing her the card. She put it with the others in the envelope. She had a very red, friendly face, her hair parted in the middle, and looked like one of those women who go into convents.

"Noldewohl built the northern town."

I knew the northern part of the town. Tall tenement buildings trying to look as bourgeois dwellings looked in 1910; the trams turned round there, broad green cars which appeared so romantic to me, just as my father looked in 1910 in a post-chaise.

"Thank you," I said, thinking: So they put up a statue to you in the old days for that.

"Do you want anything else?" asked the woman, and I said: "Yes, give me that box of notepaper, the big green one."

She opened the showcase, took the box out of the window and wiped the dust from it.

I watched her tear a strip from a roll of wrapping paper hanging on the wall, and I admired her pretty, small, pale hands, and suddenly I took out my fountain pen, unscrewed it and wrote my name on the block below where Maria Kahlisch had tried out a ball-point pen. I do not know why I did it, but I felt a need to be immortalised on that piece of paper.

"Oh," said the woman, "perhaps you'd like to fill your pen."

"No, thank you," I said, realising that I had blushed. "No, it's just been filled."

She smiled, and it seemed to me as though she understood why I had done it. I put the money on the counter, took out my cheque book, wrote out a cheque for twenty-two and a half marks and crossed it, took the envelope in which the woman had put the postcards, stuck the cards loose in my pocket and put the cheque in the envelope. It was an envelope of the cheapest kind such as one gets from the labour exchange or the police station. The ink ran when I wrote Wickweber's address. So I crossed it out and slowly rewrote it.

I took one mark from the change which the woman had returned to me and said to her: "Give me a ten-pfennig stamp, please." She opened the drawer, tore one from a sheet of stamps and I stuck it on the envelope.

I felt that I wanted to spend more money, so I left the change on the counter and looked round on the shelves. There were school notebooks such as we had used at the engineering school; I chose one bound in soft green leather and handed it to the woman to pack, and she took more wrapping paper, and I knew as soon as I took the little parcel that Hedwig would never use this little school-book.

As I walked back along the Netzmachergasse I thought the day would never come to an end; the lights were a little brighter now in the shop windows. I should have liked to spend more money, but I found nothing to buy in the shop windows. I lingered for a while before an undertaker's looking at the dark brown and black coffins which were faintly lit, and then went on and thought of Ulla as I turned into the Korbmachergasse. It would not be so easy with her as I had thought. I knew it; she had known me for a long time and she knew me well, but I knew her too. Whenever I kissed her I saw beneath the smooth, pretty girlish face the skull her father would once have—a skull wearing a green felt hat.

With her I had cheated the old man in a more cunning and lucrative way than I had done with the oven tops; we had earned more money and good money since we had sold part of the old iron

I collected with a whole gang of workers when we demolished ruins that were about to collapse. Some rooms which we reached on tall ladders had not been destroyed, and we found bathrooms and kitchens in which each oven, each boiler, each screw, was brand new, enamelled wall hooks on which towels had hung, glass shelves with lipstick and razor side by side, baths full of water in which the soapflakes had settled in a chalky sediment on the bottom, clear water in which still swam rubber animals, toys with which the children had played before being suffocated in the cellar, and I had looked in a mirror in which a man had looked a few moments before he died. A mirror in which, in rage and disgust, I smashed my own face with a hammer; silver splinters fell on the razor and the lipstick. I pulled the plug out of the bath, and the water fell down four storeys and the rubber animals sank slowly on to the chalky sediment at the bottom of the bath.

Somewhere stood a sewing machine whose needle was still stuck in a piece of brown linen which was to have been a pair of boy's shorts, and no one understood me when I tipped it through the open door down the ladder, and it broke to pieces on the rubble and the collapsed walls, but my greatest relief was to smash my own face in the mirrors we found; the silver splinters fell like tinkling fluid until Wickweber began to wonder that no mirrors ever turned up in the salvage, and another assistant was put in charge of the demolition.

But they sent me when one of the apprentices fell as he climbed in the dark up a ruined house to fetch an electric washing machine; no one could explain how he could have got up to the third floor, but he had managed it, tried to lower the machine, which was as big as a night table, on a line and was pulled down by it into the depths. His hand-cart still stood in the sunshine in the street when we arrived. The police were there, and someone who measured the length of the line with a tape measure shook his head and looked up at the open kitchen door where a broom could be seen leaning against the blue-distempered wall. The washing machine had been smashed like a nut, the drum had rolled out, but the boy lay there with no sign of injury on a heap of rotting mattresses buried in sea wrack and his mouth was as bitter as it had always been—the mouth of a starving child who did not believe in the justice of this world. His name was Alois Fruklahr and he had been only three days with Wickweber. I took him away in the hearse and a woman standing in the street asked, "Was he your brother?" and I said, "Yes, he was my brother." And that afternoon I saw Ulla dip her pen in a bottle of red ink and strike his name from the payroll. It was a straight, clean line, red as blood, red as Scharnhorst's collar, red as Iphigenia's lips, red as the ace of hearts.

. . . . .

Hedwig supported her head in her hands; her green pullover had worked up and her white forearms stood firmly on the table like bottles, between whose necks her face was imprisoned, and her face filled the round space between the narrowing necks and her eyes were dark brown with a light yellow, almost honey-coloured background and I saw my shadow fall on her eyes. But she looked past me into the corridor which I had crossed a dozen times carrying the philology folders, and of which I had only a dim, hazy recollection—red linoleum, but it could also have been dark brown, for no light fell in this corridor; a picture of her father in his student's cap and wild writing on some "onia" . . . the smell of peppermint tea, tobacco, and a music shelf on which I once read the title of the top score: "Grieg—*Anitra's Dance*."

I wished now that I had known the corridor as well as she knew it, and I racked my memory for objects I had perhaps forgotten; I cut open my memory as one opens a zip pocket to take out the coin one has felt for, which is suddenly beyond price because it is the last, the only one—the groschen for two rolls of bread, for a cigarette or a cornet of peppermint whose white wafer-like tablets with their spicy taste could stifle the hunger as one pumps air into lungs which can no longer work.

There was dust in your hand when the zip was open, flakes of wool, and fingers delved for the precious coin which you knew was a groschen but always hoped was a mark. It was only a groschen, but it was mine and beyond price. Over the entrance—I only saw it on my way out—was a picture of Christ's Flaming Heart with an oil lamp burning before it.

"You must go," said Hedwig. "I'll wait here for you. Will it take long?" she asked, without looking at me.

"This café closes at seven," I said.

"Will you be later than seven?"

"No," I said. "Certainly not. Will you be here?"

"Yes," she replied. "I shall be here. Go, now."

I laid the postcards and the stamps on the table, went back to the Judengasse, got into my car and threw the two parcels with the presents for Hedwig on to the back seat. I knew that I had always been afraid of my car just as I had been afraid of my work; but motoring was all right, just as cigarette smoking had been all right while I stood on the opposite side of the street watching her door. Motoring automatically became all right: buttons to be pressed, switches to pull, lever down, levers pushed forward. I drove the car as one drives a car in a dream; it went smoothly, quietly and easily, and I seemed to be driving through a silent world.

As I negotiated the Judengasse-Röntgenplatz cross-roads I saw Hedwig's green pullover disappearing in the dusk far behind in the Korbmachergasse and I turned back at the cross-roads and drove after her. She was running, then she spoke to a man who had crossed the street with a loaf under his arm. I stopped because I was so close, and saw the man gesticulating and explaining something to her. Hedwig ran on and I followed her slowly as she ran part of the way down the Netzmachergasse behind the stationer's where I had bought the postcards and turned into a dark alley which I did not know. She stopped running, her black handbag swung in her hand, and for a moment I switched on my headlights because I could not see the street, and then I blushed for shame as my headlights lit up the porch of a little church into which Hedwig had just gone. I felt as someone must feel when shooting a film he suddenly cuts the darkness with his arc-light and discovers a couple in close embrace.

III

I DROVE FAST ROUND THE CHURCH, TURNED ROUND and drove back to the Röntgenplatz; I was there sharp at six and saw Ulla standing outside the butcher's shop as I came out of the Tschandlerstrasse in to the Röntgenplatz. I saw her the whole time while, hemmed in by other cars, I drove slowly round the square until I could turn out of the stream and park. She was wearing her red raincoat and the black hat, and I remembered having once said how much I liked her in a red coat. I parked the car, and as I ran up to her the first thing she said was: "You can't park there; it will cost you twenty marks."

I saw by her face that she had already spoken to Wolf, and her rosy skin was dark-shadowed. Between two lumps of fat in the butcher's shop window above her head, between flower vases and marble shelves, stood a pyramid of tinned meat with bright red labels: "Corned beef." "Never mind about the car," I said. "We have so little time."

"Don't be stupid," she replied. "Give me the key. There's a free place over there."

I gave her the key and watched her get into the car, take it from the forbidden to the other side where a car had just driven away. Then I walked to the pillar-box on the corner and posted the letter to her father.

"Such stupidity," she said as she came back and handed me the key. "As though you had money to throw away."

I sighed, and thought of the eternity of a long, lifelong marriage which I had almost embarked upon with her; of the reproaches that would have fallen on my head for those thirty or forty years like stones in a well; how surprised she would be when the echo of the falling stones grew smaller, duller and more abrupt, until she heard no more echo and the stones overflowed the well, and the picture of a well full of stones pursued me as I walked with her round the corner to the Café Joos.

"Have you spoken to Wolf," I asked, and she said: "Yes." I caught her arm as we stood outside the Café Joos and said: "Do we have to talk?"

"Yes," she replied, "we have to talk." She pushed me into the café, and when I drew back the felt curtain I knew why she was so keen to sit here with me. I had been here so often with her and Wolf; already when I went with him to evening courses and later after we had taken our exams and no longer went to the engineering school the Café Joos had been our meeting place. We had drunk innumerable cups of coffee here together and eaten innumerable ices, and I saw from Ulla's smile as she stood beside me looking for a free table that she thought she had inveigled me into a trap. Here were the walls, the tables, the chairs, the odours and the faces of the waitresses—they were all on her side; here she would fight with me on a ground where the wings were her wings, but she did not know that these years—it must have been three or four—had been erased from my memory although I had sat here with her yesterday. I had cast the years away as one casts away a souvenir which one once kept because it seemed so important and valuable—the bit of rock taken from the top of Mont Blanc to remind one of the moment when one suddenly knew what it meant. It made one giddy, this grey chip of stone as big as a match-box but which looked like a million tons of rock on this earth—and one suddenly dropped it out of the train between the rails where it was lost among the slag.

On the previous evening we had been there late; she had fetched me after Mass and I had washed my hands in the toilet, for they were still dirty from my work. I had eaten a pie and drunk some wine and somewhere under the notes in my pocket must still lie the receipt the girl had given me. Six marks, fifty-eight pfennigs must stand on it and I saw the girl who had given it to me hanging the evening newspapers on the rack.

"Shall we sit down?" asked Ulla.

"Yes, let's sit down."

Frau Joos stood behind the counter arranging pralines with a pair of silver tongs in a glass dish. I had hoped that we should avoid being greeted by Frau Joos, but she set store by this, for she liked "young people." Now she came from behind the counter, stretched out both hands and pressed my wrist because I was holding the car key and my hat. "How nice to see you again," she cried, and I knew that I blushed and looked with embarrassment at her pretty slanting eyes, in which I could read how much women liked me. Her daily contact with pralines, which was her department, had made her resemble them; she looked exactly like a praline—sweet, clean and appetising—and her delicate fingers were always a little splayed from constantly using the silver tongs. She was small and hopped like a bird, and the two white streaks at her temples reminded me of the marzipan strips in certain pralines; in her small egg-shaped skull resided the whole praline topography of our city; she knew exactly which praline each woman preferred, how to give pleasure, and so she was adviser to all beaux and the confidante of big business men who wished to send little gifts to the wives of their best customers on feast days. From the use of certain combinations of pralines she knew all the forthcoming divorces and those that had already taken place. She discovered new mixtures which with great skill she made fashionable.

She gave Ulla her hand, and smiled. I put the car key in my pocket and she shook hands with me in turn.

I looked closer into those pretty eyes and tried to imagine how she would have spoken to me had I come seven years ago and asked her for a loaf. And I saw those eyes narrow, become hard and dry like a goose's, and I saw those enchanting, delicately splayed fingers shrink to claws, saw those soft, well-tended hands grow wrinkled and yellow from greed, and I withdrew mine so hastily that she recoiled and returned to her counter shaking her head. Her face now looked like a praline which had fallen into the mud and whose filling slowly trickled into the gutter, no longer a sweet but a sour filling.

Ulla drew me away and we walked past the occupied tables across the russet-red carpet to the back of the café, where she must have spotted two empty chairs. There was no table free, only these two vacant chairs at a table for three. A man sat there smoking a cigar and reading a paper; when he exhaled a thin, pale grey smoke came through the ash and little particles of ash fell on his dark suit.

"Here?" I asked.

"They're the only places vacant," said Ulla.

"I meant that perhaps it might be better to go to another café."

She threw a glance of hatred at the man, looked round, and I saw a triumphant gleam appear in her eyes as a man in the corner stood up and helped his wife into a light blue coat. I felt once more as I walked behind her that it was incredibly important to her that our conversation should take place here. She threw her handbag on the chair on which a box of shoes belonging to the woman with the light blue coat still lay, and the woman picked up her box with a shake of the head and joined her husband, who stood between the tables paying the waitress.

Ulla collected the dirty crockery and sat down on a chair in the corner. I sat down on the chair opposite, took out my own cigarettes and looked at the dirty plate with the remains of buttermilk, cherry stones and the grey milky slops in one of the coffee cups.

"I should have known it," said Ulla, "when I

watched you in the factory through the glass wall that separates the counting house from the works. How you associated with the little work-girls to get a piece of their breakfast bread. One was an ugly little runt, one of the armature winders; she was slightly rickety and had an unhealthy, spotty face; she gave you half her bread and jam, and I noticed how you stuffed it into your mouth."

"But what you don't know is that I kissed her and took her to the cinema and held her hand in the dark, and she died at the time I passed my exams and I gave a whole week's wages for flowers to put on her grave. I hope that she has forgiven me for that half a slice of bread and jam."

Ulla looked at me in silence, pushed the dirty crockery farther away and I pushed it back, because a plate had almost fallen on the floor.

"You didn't even think it necessary," I went on, "to send a wreath to her funeral, not even a letter of sympathy to her parents. I suppose you merely drew a clean straight line in red ink through her name on the payroll."

The waitress came, cleared the plates and cups on a tray and said: "Coffee?"

"No, none for me, thank you," I replied.

"I'll have some," said Ulla.

"What about you?" asked the girl.

"Oh, anything," I said wearily.

"Bring Mr. Fendrich a peppermint tea," ordered Ulla.

"Yes," I said, "I'll have that."

"I'm sorry," said the girl. "We haven't any peppermint tea, only Indian."

"All right, Indian then," I said, and the girl left.

I looked at Ulla and was surprised, as I had so often been, to notice that her pretty sensuous mouth was as small and thin as the lines she drew with a ruler.

I took off my wrist-watch and put it down on the table; it was ten minutes past six, and I would leave not a minute later than a quarter to seven.

"I would have gladly paid the twenty marks to talk to you for two minutes longer; I would have gladly given you the extra two minutes as a farewell present, like two particularly costly flowers, but you robbed yourself of them. These two minutes were worth twenty marks to me."

"Yes," she replied, "you've become a fine gentleman, who gives away flowers at ten marks the bloom."

"Yes," I said. "I thought it worth while since we have never given each other anything. Never, eh?"

"No," she said, "we have never given each other presents. It has been impressed upon me that one must earn presents, and I never felt that you had earned one, nor do I ever seem to have earned one."

"No," I replied. "And the only thing I wanted to give you, although you hadn't deserved it, was that single present you did not take. And when we went out together," I went on gently, "we never forgot to get a bill for the tax inspector, alternately one for you and the other for me. Had there been a question of receipts for kisses, you would have filed them in a card index."

"But there are receipts for kisses," she replied, "as you'll see for yourself one day."

The girl brought Ulla's coffee and my tea, and the ceremony seemed to last for an eternity—the arrangement of the plates, the cups, the milk jugs and sugar bowls, the tea cosy and then another little plate on which lay a pair of silver clips holding a small slice of lemon between its teeth.

Ulla was silent, and I was afraid that she would scream. I had heard her scream once when her father refused her a power of attorney. Time stood still; it was thirteen minutes past six.

"Put that watch away, damn you," said Ulla softly.

I covered the watch with the menu.

I felt that I must have heard, seen and smelt it all countless times, like the records the people who lived above me put on every evening at a certain time—like a film which is projected for one in hell, always the same one—this odour in the air of coffee, sweat, scent, liqueur and cigarettes; what I said, what Ulla said, had already been said countless times, and it was no use, the words tasted false on the tongue. It resembled what I had told Father of the black market and of my hunger—as soon as you uttered it it was no longer true—and suddenly I recalled the scene when Helene Frenkel had given me the bread and jam so clearly that I could taste the cheap red jam, and I longed for Hedwig and the dark green shadows of the bridge beneath which Jurgen Brolaski was drowned.

"I don't quite understand," said Ulla, "because I don't understand that there are things you don't do for money. Or has she money?"

"No," I replied, "she has no money, but she knows that I once stole. One of you must have told someone who repeated it to her brother. Even Wolf reminded me of it again."

"Yes," she said, "it was a good thing he did. You have become so arrogant that you are probably beginning to forget that you once stole stove tops to buy cigarettes."

"And bread," I said. "The bread that you and your father did not give me. Only Wolf gave me some, sometimes. He did not know the meaning of hunger, but he always gave me his bread when we worked together. I think," I went on gently, "that had you but once given me a piece of bread it would be impossible for me to sit here and talk to you like this."

"We always paid more than the standard rate, and everyone who worked for us got his allowance and a ticket for free soup at midday."

"Yes," I said, "you always paid more than the standard rate, and everyone who worked for you got his allowance and a ticket for free soup at midday."

"You scoundrel," she cried, "you ungrateful scoundrel."

I took the menu off my watch, but since it was not yet half-past six I covered it up again.

"Look through the wages sheets again," I replied, "the lists you kept, read the names once more, aloud and reverently, as one reads a litany, call them out and say after each name, 'Forgive us,' then add the name, multiply the number of names by a thousand loaves—the result is in thousands—then you have the number of curses that lie on your father's banking account. The arithmetical unit is the bread, the bread of those early years, which lie in my memory as though beneath a deep fog; the soup which was issued to us rumbled dully in our bellies; it rose hot and sour in us, when we rattled home at night in the tram. It was the belching of impotence and the only fun we had was the hatred—the hatred," I repeated softly, "which has long since flown out of me as when a belcher presses hard on his belly. Ah, Ulla," I said quietly, looking at her in the eyes for the first time, "do you really want to persuade me, to make me believe that it was all done with soup and a little extra wages—is that what you want? Just think of the big rolls of greaseproof paper!"

She stirred her coffee, returned my gaze and offered her cigarettes. I took one, gave her a match and lit my own.

"It is a matter of indifference, that you told these people of my legendary theft, but you're not seriously trying to make me believe that all of us, all of us on your wage list, did not from time to time need a few extra slices of bread?"

She was still silent, staring over my head. "When I went home," I said, "I used to pinch my father's books to buy myself bread, books he loved and had collected, books for which he had gone hungry as a student. Books for which he had paid the price of twenty loaves I sold for the price of half a loaf; that is the interest we received: minus two hundred to minus infinity."

"But we too," said Ulla calmly, "paid interest, interests of which you know nothing."

"Yes, you paid them, and you did not know how high the percentage was, but I took the books at random, choosing the thick ones; my father had so many that I thought he would never notice; only later did I learn that he knew each of them as a shepherd knows his sheep, and one of these books was small and shabby and ugly and I sold it for the price of a box of matches, and later I learnt that it was worth a truck-load of loaves. Later my father blushed as he told me that I had better leave the sale of the books to him. And he sold them himself, and sent me the money, and I bought myself bread. . . ."

She recoiled as I said the word "bread," and now I was sorry for her. "Hit me if you like," she said, "throw the tea in my face, go on talking, you who never wanted to talk, but please don't mention the word 'bread' again, spare me the sound of it . . . please." And I said: "I'm sorry, I won't mention it again." I gave a start as I looked at her again; the Ulla who sat there changed under my words, under my gaze, under the effect of the small hand that went forward ruthlessly under the menu. She was no more the one for whom my words had been meant. I thought she would talk a lot and to a certain extent be right, but now I had spoken a lot and I had been right to a certain extent.

She looked at me, and I knew that later, on the way home, past the dark workshop to her father's house, when she skirted the bushes on the gravel path under the elder tree, that she would do what I least expected of her, that she would weep—and I did not know the weeping Ulla.

I thought that she would have gloated, but now I had won and I felt the sour taste of victory on my tongue.

She had not touched her coffee; she played with her spoon, and I was horrified by her voice when she said: "I would gladly give you a blank cheque if you could remove the curses from our bank account. It is good to know that you brooded on these things all these years, counted the curses without telling me."

"I haven't thought of it all these years," I replied. "It's something else; today perhaps, not until I got here, it struck me for the first time. You pour red dye into a spring to find out how far its veins reach, but it can be years before you find the red-tinged water in some unexpected place. Today the streams bleed, and only today do I know where my red dye tarried."

"You may be right," she said. "I too know today for the first time that money means nothing to me; it would not worry me if I gave you a second blank cheque and a cash payment as well, and you could draw as much as you like and it would not hurt me, and I always thought that it would hurt me. Perhaps you are right, but it's all too late."

"Yes," I replied, "it's too late; one sees the horse pass the winning-post on which one wanted to stake a thousand marks—the filled-out betting slip is in your hand, the white slip that would have been worth a fortune had you handed it in, but you did not hand it in, and the ticket is useless; it is not even worth while preserving as a souvenir."

"One still has the thousand left," she argued. "But you would probably throw the thousand marks with the slip into the gutter."

"Yes," I said, "I think that is what I would do." I poured the milk into my cold tea, pressed the lemon and saw how the milk thickened and sank in yellowish blobs. I offered my cigarettes to Ulla, but she shook her head. I had no wish to smoke, and put the packet away. I raised the menu a little from my watch and saw that it was ten minutes to seven. I covered my watch again quickly with the menu, but she had seen it and said: "Go, now; I'll stay here."

"Can I drive you home?" I asked.

"No, I'm going to stay here. Go, now."

But I did not stir, and she said, "Give me your

hand," and I gave it to her. She held it tightly for a moment without looking at it, let it fall suddenly before I had thought she would release it, and my hand banged against the edge of the table. . . .

"I'm sorry," she said. "I didn't mean to do that."

I felt a stab of pain in my hand, but I believed her when she said that she had not done it on purpose.

"I've often watched your hands, how you held the tools, how you caught hold of the machinery, how you dismantled apparatus that you hardly knew, studied your way of working, and re-assembled it. One could see that you were made for this profession and that you loved it—and that it was better to let you earn your bread than to give it to you."

"I don't love it," I said. "I hate it as a boxer hates fighting."

"Go, now," she repeated, "go." And I went without another word, without looking round to the counter, and then turned round and paid the girl who was standing between the tables for the coffee and the tea.

IV

IT WAS DARK AND STILL MONDAY AS I DROVE back to the Judengasse. I drove fast. But it was already seven and I had forgotten that the Nudelbreite was closed to cars at seven, and I drove aimlessly around it through dark unrepaired streets until I came to the church where I had last seen Hedwig.

It suddenly struck me that both Hedwig and Ulla had told me to go.

I drove once more past the stationer's and the undertaker's in the Korbmachergasse, and it gave me a shock when I saw that there was no light burning in the café. I was going to drive past into the Judengasse when at the last moment I caught sight of Hedwig's green pullover in the café entrance, and I braked so hard that the car skidded on to the parapet of clay where the street had been torn up and repaved, and my left hand banged against the door handle. Both hands hurt me as I got out and went over to Hedwig. She stood there like the girls who sometimes accosted me when I went through the dark streets at night, without a coat, in her light green pullover, a white face beneath dark hair, and the whiter—painfully white—slender leaf of her throat; her mouth looked as though it had been painted black.

She neither moved nor spoke, did not even look at me, and I took her by the hand without a word and dragged her to the car.

A crowd had gathered, for the screech of my brakes had been like a trumpet call in the silent street, and I quickly opened the door, pushed Hedwig inside, slipped into the driving seat and drove away. Not until we were past the station did I have time to look at her. She was deathly pale and sat there rigid as a statue.

I pulled up under a street lamp. It was a dark street and the circle of light from the lamp fell on a lawn, cutting a round piece of turf out of the darkness; it was silent all around me.

"A man spoke to me," said Hedwig, and I was terrified because she still looked straight ahead like a statue. "A man. He wanted to take me with him or to go with me, and he looked so nice. He was carrying a briefcase and his teeth were a little yellow from nicotine; he must have been thirty-five, but he was nice."

"Hedwig," I said, but she did not look at me until I took her by the arm, then she turned her head and said softly, "Drive me home," and I noticed how naturally she had slipped into the *"du."*

"Yes, I'll take you home," I said. "Oh God!"

"No, wait a minute," she said. And she looked at me as directly as I had once looked at her, but now I was afraid to look at her. I started to sweat and I felt the pain in both my hands—and this day, this Monday, appeared to me unbearably long, too long for a single day, and I knew that I should never have left her room. I had discovered the country and had not yet run up my flag. It was a beautiful land, but it was strange, as beautiful as it was strange.

"Oh God," she murmured softly. "I'm so happy that you're nicer than he, much nicer. The baker was not as nice as he looked. At seven o'clock punctually he threw me out. You shouldn't have been late. Drive on, now," she said. I drove slowly and the dark streets through which I drove seemed to be paths across a moor into which a car could sink at any minute. I drove carefully as though I were carrying explosives, and I heard her voice, felt her hand on my arm, and felt as a man must feel when he stands before his Maker on Judgment Day.

"I nearly went with him," she said. "I don't know how long he would have persisted, but he gave up. He wanted to marry me, wanted to get a divorce. He had children and he was nice, but he ran away when the headlights of your car lit up the street. For a single moment he stood at my side whispering nervously like people who are in a hurry, and he was in a hurry—a single minute and I lived a whole lifetime at the side of this man. I fell into his arms and out of his arms again; I bore his children, darned his socks, took his briefcase when he came home at night and kissed him when the door closed behind him; I was pleased with his new set of teeth, and when he got a rise we celebrated; there were cakes and we went to the cinema and he bought me a new hat as red as cherry jam; and he did with me what you wanted to do with me, and I liked his clumsy caresses; I saw him change his clothes, his Sunday best became his everyday suit when he got a new Sunday best, and when this wore out he got a new suit and the children grew up and more hats as red as cherry jam, and I forbade them to do what I was always forbidden to do—to go out in the rain; I forbade them for the same reason that I myself had been forbidden—because clothes get ruined so quickly in the rain. . . . I was his widow and I received a letter of condolence from his firm. He was accountant in a chocolate factory, and in the evening he told me how much his firm made on the 'Youssopoff praline'; they made a huge profit, and he told me not to mention it, but I did mention it; in the dairy next morning I betrayed how much his firm made on the 'Youssopoff praline.' He had only to hold out for a few minutes, but he did not hold out. He ran off like a hare when your car turned into the street. 'I am not ill-bred, Fräulein,' he said to me."

I drove even slower, for my left hand had begun to ache, and my right was a little swollen. I drove into the Judengasse as slowly as if I had been driving on a bridge that might collapse.

"What do you want here?" asked Hedwig. "Are you going to stop here?"

I looked at her nervously as the man must have looked at her.

"We can't go up to my room because Hilde Kamenz is waiting for me. I saw the light in my room and her car outside my door."

I drove slowly past the front door, the brown front door whose picture I should see again when it came out of the dark room—row after row of front doors like sheets of new stamps when they leave the State printing press.

A burgundy-red car stood outside this door.

I looked at Hedwig and raised my eyebrows.

"Hilde Kamenz is my father's relative. Drive round the corner. I noticed from my window that there's a gap in the houses in the next street. I saw the dark pavement there with the brown clay parapet in the middle and saw you lying dead, for I was afraid that you would not return."

I turned and drove into the Korbmachergasse so slowly that I felt I should never drive fast again. The gap in the houses was just past the bakery, and we looked at the back of the house in which Hedwig lived. Tall trees masked a part of it, but we could see the whole array of windows; on the ground floor the window was dark, but brightly lit on the first floor, and there was also a light on the second floor. "My room," she said. "If she opened the window we could see her silhouette. You would have fallen blindly into this trap, and she would have taken us off to her flat, a beautiful flat, as they all are when they appear to be accidental. But you see at the first sight that the accident was only carefully arranged, and you feel as you feel when you come out of a cinema still in the grip of the film and someone says outside the cloakroom as they leave: 'Not a bad film but the music was poor.' There she is. . . ."

I looked up at her window and saw the silhouette of a woman wearing a pointed hat, and although I could not see her eyes I sensed that she was looking at our car with the eyes of a woman who wants to bring some order into other people's lives. "Drive home," said Hedwig, "drive. . . . I'm so afraid that if she spots us and we fall into her hands we shall spend the whole evening in that flat drinking wonderful tea and we can't even hope that her children will wake up and demand their mother's attention, for the children have been regimented and sleep from seven in the evening until seven in the morning. Drive on . . . and her husband is not there, he's gone away; he's building flats at a huge fee somewhere for other people to look as though they had been created by accident. Drive on!"

I drove through the Korbmachergasse and the Netzmachergasse, slowly crossed the Nudelbreite, drove round the Röntgenplatz, glanced in the butcher's shop window where the corned beef pyramid stood, and thought once more of Ulla and the years with her. These years had shrunk like a shirt which has not stood up to the washing —but the time since midday, since Hedwig's arrival, was another time.

I was tired and my eyes hurt, and as I drove down the Münchnerstrasse I was almost alone on the right-hand side and moved over to the left to pass the cars as they hooted and passed each other triumphantly. There must have been a boxing match or a bicycle race in the stadium. I constantly had the headlights of the oncoming cars in my eyes; the harsh light hurt my eyes and at moments I groaned. It was like running the gauntlet of an endless line of bright spears, and each time one of them pierced me and tormented me with its light. I was lashed with light, and I thought of the years when I woke up in the morning and I hated the light; for two years the idea of progress had stimulated me, and I had got up every morning at half-past five, drunk a cup of bitter tea, wrestled with formulae or pottered about in my little cellar workshop, polished and assembled, tried constructions which often overloaded the electricity power until the cables smouldered and I heard voices upstairs screaming as the coffee percolator fused. My alarm clock stood on the writing-desk or the working-bench, and not until it rang at eight o'clock did I go upstairs, take a bath and fetch my breakfast from my landlady's kitchen. I had been working for two and a half hours before most people started to breakfast. Although I had hated and sometimes loved these two and a half hours I never missed them. But often when I breakfasted in my sunny bedroom I had felt the lashing of the light as I felt it now.

The Münchnerstrasse is a long street and I was glad when we passed the stadium.

Hedwig hesitated for a brief second when we stopped. I opened the door for her, took her hand and ran up the steps ahead of her.

It was half-past seven and I felt that eternity must be a Monday. It was just eleven hours since I had left the house.

I listened in the corridor, heard my landlady's children laughing at their supper, and I saw now why my feet had been so heavy as I ran up the steps: lumps of clay had stuck to my shoes and Hedwig's shoes were covered with clay from the parapet in the middle of the Korbmachergasse.

"I'm not going to put on the light," I said to Hedwig as we went into my room. My eyes were very painful.

"No," she said, "don't put on the light," and I closed the door behind her.

A soft light fell into the room from the window on the opposite side of the street, and on the desk I could see the slips of paper on which Frau Brotig had written the calls that had come through for me. The slips were held down by a stone; I took the stone, weighed it in my hand like a javelin, opened the window and threw it into the front garden. I heard it rolling in the dark until it hit the dustbin. I left the window open, and looked at the slips in the dark—there were seven calls. I tore them up and threw the fragments into the waste-paper basket.

"Have you any soap?" asked Hedwig. "I'd like to wash my hands. The water in my room was full of rust and dirt."

"The soap is on the left on the lower shelf," I replied.

I took a cigarette from my pocket, and as I lit it and turned round to put the match in the ash-tray I caught sight of Hedwig's face in the mirror. Her lips were like the lips printed on the paper pad on which I dried my razor blades. There was a rush of water as she washed her hands, and I heard her rinsing them. I was waiting for something, and I knew what I had been waiting for when there was a gentle knock on my door. It was my landlady. I went quickly to the door, half opened it and slipped out to join her in the passage.

She had taken off her apron and was folding it, and now, for the first time in the four years I had lived in her house, I saw that she resembled Frau Wietzel—only a little, but there was a resemblance —and now I also saw for the first time how old she was . . . forty . . . perhaps more. She had a cigarette in her mouth and was shaking her apron to hear whether there were any matches in her pocket. She had none, and I felt in vain in my own pockets. I had left mine in the bedroom, and I gave her a light from my burning cigarette; she inhaled deeply and returned it to me. She smoked as usually only men smoke, inhaling deeply with great relief.

"What a day," she said. "In the end I did not write down any more, there seemed no point since you had disappeared. Why did you forget the poor woman in the Kurbelstrasse?"

I shrugged my shoulders and looked into her grey, rather slanting eyes. "Did you remember the flowers?"

"No, I forgot them."

She fell silent, fiddled with her cigarette as she leaned against the wall, and I knew that it was difficult for her to say what she wanted to say. I wanted to help her but could not find the right words. She ran her left hand over her forehead and said: "Your supper is in the kitchen." But my supper was always in the kitchen, and I said, "Thank you," and looked past her and said gently into the wallpaper: "Say it, then."

"I don't like to," she stammered. "It disturbs me . . . it torments me to have to tell you that I don't want the girl to spend the night with you."

"Did you see her?" I asked.

"No, but I heard the two of you. It was so quiet that I suddenly knew everything. Is she going to stay with you?"

"Yes," I replied. "She is my wife."

"And where did you marry her?" She did not smile, and I looked into the wallpaper, into the orange-coloured triangles. I did not reply.

"Ah," she said gently. "You know I don't like saying it, but I can't allow such things. I can't, and I must tell you, and not only tell you, it's no use; I . . ."

"There are special licences," I said. "Just the same as there are emergency baptisms."

"Yes," she said, "those are tricks; we're not in the wilds or in the desert where there are no priests."

"We are both in the desert and in the wilderness, and far and wide I see no priest who would marry us." And I closed my eyes, for they hurt terribly from the glare of the headlights, and I was tired, dead tired, and both my hands ached. The orange triangles danced before my eyes.

"Or do you know one?" I asked.

"No," said Frau Brotig, "I don't know one."

I took the ashtray from the chair by the telephone, stubbed out my cigarette and held it out to her; she flicked the ash off the cigarette and took the ashtray from me.

I had never been so weary in my life. The orange triangles pierced my eyes like thorns, and I hated her husband who bought such things because they were what he called "modern." "You should give a little thought to your father. You still love him, don't you?"

"Yes," I said, "I love him, and I often thought of him today." And I thought once more of Father, saw him writing in blood-red ink on a huge pad: "Talk to the boy."

I caught sight of Hedwig first in my landlady's eyes—a dark patch in this friendly grey. I did not turn round but felt her hand on my shoulder and her breath, and I smelt that she had made up her lips with a sweet-smelling lipstick.

"This is Frau Brotig," I said, "and this is Hedwig." Hedwig put out her hand to the landlady and I saw how large Hedwig's hands were, how white and strong as Frau Brotig's lay in hers.

We all fell silent, and I heard a tap dripping in the kitchen, the footsteps of a man in the street with the joy of work ended in his steps, and I kept on smiling inanely. Why? For I was too tired to make the little move of my lips to take the smile off my face.

Frau Brotig replaced the ashtray on the stool below the telephone and threw down her apron; the cigarette ash rose in the air and the particles sank like powder on the dark blue carpet. She lit a new cigarette from the old one and said: "Sometimes I forget how young you are, but now go and save me the trouble of throwing you out. Go. . . ."

I turned round and pulled Hedwig by the arm into my bedroom. I felt in the dark for my car key, found it on my writing-desk, and we made our way down the stairs again in our muddy shoes. I was glad that I had not put the car in the garage but had left it in the street. My left hand was still stiff and swollen and my right hand ached from banging it on the marble edge of the café table. I was tired and hungry and I drove slowly back into town. Hedwig was silent; she held a hand mirror up to her face, and I saw that she was looking at her lips, for she took the lipstick out of her bag and made them up slowly and firmly.

The Nudelbreite was still closed, and it was not yet eight o'clock when I passed the church in the Netzmachergasse, drove through the Korbmachergasse and pulled up in the house gap opposite the bakery.

The light in Hedwig's room was still burning. I drove on and saw the red car still standing in front of the door and drove round the whole block until we came back to the gap in the Korbmachergasse. It was silent and dark. We, too, were silent. The hunger in my belly came and went in spasms like the waves of an earthquake. I suddenly realised that the cheque I had sent to Wickweber's was not covered, and I thought that Hedwig had not once asked about my profession, that she did not even know my Christian name. The pain in my hands grew worse, and when I closed my tortured eyes for a few seconds the orange triangles still danced before them.

The light in Hedwig's room would go out on this Monday, which still had four hours left to run.

The sound of the red car's engine would die away, and I already thought I heard it vanishing into the night, leaving behind it silence and darkness. We would go up the steps, open the doors gently and close them. I looked once more at Hedwig's lips; once more she painted them with a long slow gesture as though they were not red enough, and I already knew now what I should only learn later.

. . . . .

Never before had I known that I was immortal and yet how mortal I was; I heard the screams of the children who had been murdered in Bethlehem, and in their screams I heard the death cry of Fruklahr, a scream inaudible except to my ear alone; I smelt the breath of the lions which rent the martyrs, felt their claws like thorns in my flesh; I tasted the salt tang of the sea, bitter drops from the deepest depths, and I looked into pictures which overflowed their frames like water flooding the bank—landscapes I had never seen, faces I had never known—and I plunged through these pictures to Hedwig's face, rebounded off Brolaski and Helene Frenkel and Fruklahr, plunged through these faces again to Hedwig, and I knew that her face was eternal, that I should see it again, with a cloth before this face that she would suddenly tear off in order to show it to Grommig. Hedwig's face that I could not see with my eyes because the night was so dark; but I no longer needed eyes to see her.

Pictures came out of the dark room. I saw myself like a stranger bending over Hedwig and I was jealous of myself; I saw the man who had spoken to her, his yellow teeth, his briefcase, saw Mozart smiling at Fräulein Klintick, the piano teacher who lived next to us, and the woman from the Kurbelstrasse wept into all the pictures and it was still Monday, and I knew that I should never progress. I wanted to go back; I did not know where, but to go back.

Keel, Achill,
July-September 1955.